Hangdog

Christopher L. Malone

First published in paperback by
Michael Terence Publishing in 2017
www.mtp.agency

ISBN 9781549904219

For Chasi.

My Dearest Marcie,

Who knew we'd ever get to see my name in print? You are a huge credit to that, and I will never forget your ardent support.

Love and friendship always,

Hangdog

Christopher L. Malone

One: Pick Up

All of this is mutual.

We're two people sitting in a bar, and neither one of us is interested in being alone tonight. We can't come right out and say it though, because that's not how anyone comes up in this world. Despite whatever progress our generation may lay claim to, we're still saddled with the same social mores, and we drink to continue on with the same dance that's been done for ages. She knows what role she wants to play, and I know mine; the expectation is for me to continue to push the momentum forward, and I do so with a seemingly casual question.

"So why don't you tell me something interesting about yourself?

I don't ask her this question because I'm really interested in her answer, even though I know that the nature of the question helps me to come off as a sensitive guy who isn't the least bit insincere. Really, I'm only asking the question because I know that when she's done taking her time to come up with a thoughtful response, she'll flip the question back over to me, and I already know what I'm going to say.

Her reaction's pretty much textbook, considering the number of times I've seen it in other women. As soon as the words leave my lips, she giggles and says something about putting her on the spot while she looks up and away, twirling a lock of her red hair between her index and middle fingers. I know she's being flirtatious, and I'm okay with that. I'm being flirtatious, too. This conversation is the first stage in a long night of cat and mouse, and I'm almost 100% sure at this point that one of us is going home with the other; I've never been too picky about where the night ends.

"Well, she says, and she really draws out the last syllable, "I've got a heart-shaped birthmark on my left hip...

I raise my eyebrows and act like this is *big*, but really, I've been there before. She's forward, and it's just another thing of hers that I'm okay with. Some women are coy, just like some men are bashful, and sometimes a human being just wants to get laid, or at the very least, not sleep alone. There're all kinds of speeds out there, and I've never had a problem with going fast or slow. I just try to play it cool.

I take a drink from the long neck that's been collecting condensation in my hand and look away from her, like I'm shocked and trying to process what she's told me, and this makes her giggle even more, like she's pleased with herself and the effect that this revelation has had on me.

“Damn,” I say to her, and I look at her with a bemused smile before turning back for another sip of beer. “Is it really in the shape of a heart?” I ask her after another short, incredulous pause.

“Yep!” she says brightly, and I can see that she is thoroughly pleased with herself.

“Well,” I say, and she doesn't realize that I'm mimicking the way she draws out this word, “I've always been a pretty visual guy...”

She glares at me playfully, because she knows where I'm going with this, and she doesn't bat an eye when I ask her, “Do you think I could see it?”

“What, you don't believe me?” she asks, regarding me in faux-indignation.

“Hey,” I say with my hands up in surrender. “You can't blame a guy for asking. It's not every day you meet a woman with heart-shaped birthmarks on her body.”

“It better not be,” she says, sliding her hips toward me while she leans back in her bar stool. “Besides,” she adds, “it's only the one birthmark,” and she slides her thumbs into the waistband of her jeans, pulling down the left side just enough to reveal the tops of her lacy pink underwear and an asymmetrical brown splotch that vaguely resembles a heart. If I were feeling like an asshole, I'd tell her that she might want to get that checked for cancer, because melanoma's a bitch, and it wouldn't be the first time I've hit the self-destruct button on a night for the sake of a profane laugh. Tonight, however, I am mildly drunk and horny, and I know that the appropriate response is to appear dazed, like I've never seen such a thing before, because I honestly haven't, and say:

"Wow, you really weren't kidding."

"See," she says cheerfully, "Told ya so!" and she releases her waist band and turns to her own drink, taking a small sip while appearing satisfied with herself. It's an indulgent moment and it passes quickly, before she finally flips the question back over to me. "So, what about you?" she asks. "Tell me something interesting about yourself."

This is my moment, but I can't jump on it immediately. It would sound too scripted, and even though it is, *she* doesn't need to know that. Instead, I cringe, make a face like I'm experiencing self-doubt, and I mutter something like, "Eh..."

"Oh, come on!" she prods, "I answered the question." She pouts slightly after saying this and she adds, "Fair is fair."

"I don't know," I say to her with a sideways glance, "It's kinda stupid, but..." and I can see now that she's hooked on to what I'm going to say next.

"Well?" she asks.

"*Well*," I repeat, "I guess I've always been pretty good about keeping out of trouble, so sometimes I like to pretend that I'm a criminal, just to see what it might be like to have that mindset."

She's got a look on her face that suggests she's extremely amused by this revelation, and I know that at this point I can say no wrong. Some women never lose their sense of apprehension, but some warm up to you quickly, and in this case, she's made the decision that I am essentially a decent person. After a moment, her look becomes meaningful, like she's genuinely curious, and asks, "So, like, what does that mean? How do you pretend to be something like that?"

"I like to case places," I say with a shrug of my shoulders, and I take a confident swig of my beer, knowing full well she's going to follow me on this train of logic.

"You *case* a place?" she asks, and I can see that she's unsure of what the lingo means.

"Yeah," I say, totally sure of myself, "like in those old heist movies. A guy walks into a place, whatever the target is, and he scopes out the security, and where all the cameras are and shit."

"And you do this for fun?" she asks, half-amused, but half in disbelief.

"As a hobby," I reply in slight defense, and I wonder what comes next. The whole moment turns on her response. If she wants, she can dismiss the whole conversation, take her drink and look for her friends to tell them about the creep hitting on her the bar with the lame come on. It happens sometimes, and if it happens tonight I can save face and just shrug my shoulders like I'm not bothered by it. What happens instead though is what I always hope for when I go through these motions. When she opens her mouth to speak, she raises one inquisitive eyebrow, and gives me the perfect form of permission to continue things.

"Prove it," she says, and she's glaring at me slightly now, like if I can't, she knows I'm full of shit and she can walk away laughing without looking back. It's challenging and I can feel myself becoming slightly aroused just by the way her eyes are digging into me.

A smug grin creeps over my face and my lips move without hesitation. "Okay, so, before you walk into the bar, I know you've seen that small camera they have mounted directly over the door frame, right?" She nods in affirmation, and I continue along. "Now see, that's an easy one, because you figure that's just so the bar has an eye on everyone coming in and coming out. What most people *don't* notice is the cameras they got high up on the outside corners so they can see what's happening on the sidewalks and streets outside of here." Her look softens, becoming quizzical, and she's wearing the smallest grin. "You want to go outside and check, don't you?" I ask her.

"Just real quick!" she says brightly, and she hops off her

barstool and goes out and around the corner. I take the opportunity to order two more drinks, and when she comes back she has a very pleased look on her face. "You know, I've seen the one over the door that you were talking about, but I've never noticed those other ones! That's so wild..."

"Yeah, but that's not all," I say, and she hops back onto her barstool to hear the rest of what I've got to say. "If you look behind the bar, over here is a small camera mounted directly to our right that looks over the bartender's shoulder when they're at the cash register." I point at it with my finger, and she follows the sight line.

"I would've never spotted that," she says, and it's clear that she's fully committed to playing out the conversation in full.

"They probably say it's there to catch anyone in a stick up," I continue, "but I think it's more likely that they're there to make sure the bar staff isn't stealing from the register."

"Wow, good call," she says, and asks, "Any others to note?"

"Well, as far as the bathrooms are concerned, I know there aren't any cameras in the actual rooms themselves, but there *is* one to the left of them, just outside of both doors to make sure that boys are going in the boys' room and girls are going in the girls' room. At least, that's what I think they're there for."

Her eyes have been following my directions this entire time, and it's nice to see that she's not turned off by what I've said. It's always a risk when you lay this particular line, but when it hits, it really snags. After she glances at the camera by the bathroom doors, she shoots me a coy look.

"How do you know there're no cameras in the ladies' room?" she asks.

"Like you've never gone into the wrong restroom before," I quip, and she laughs. I smile back at her and we both take a long drink from the two new bottles the bartender has placed in front of us during my explanation of his business's surveillance, allowing a comfortable lull to settle into the conversation. I can see that she's working up to something, and it's this point in the night that's most exciting to me. The line played, and the foundation has been laid, but until you're in someone's bedroom with the lights out, there's always enough room for doubt, and it's fun to see where things might go.

"So," she asks, "how come you never pull off any big robberies if you're so good at thinking like a criminal?"

"A couple of reasons," I respond.

"And they are?"

"Well, for starters," I say, "I've already got a job, so I don't really need the money, and I certainly don't need the jail time. Besides that fact, I think I'm *just* ethnic enough to know I'd be feeding into a stereotype, and I'd rather not. It's bad enough as it is."

She'd been laughing at the line about jail time, but the laughter dies off when I bring up ethnicity. "Just ethnic enough," she echoes with a hint of confusion, and it brings to my face a genuine smile.

"You can't tell?" I ask her earnestly, and I'm interested in her response. She's incredibly pale, and has the look of someone who takes pride in their Irish heritage; green eyes, fair skin, and hair the color of burnt orange. She could pass as a human flag for her nationality.

She fumbles with a response, and it's kind of endearing. "I don't know that it's something I would notice, honestly..."

"Nah, it's cool," I reply, cutting her off, and she looks mildly relieved. "Most people don't notice. I'm pretty olive-skinned, so more often than not people are guessing that I'm Latin or something, which is fine by me. My mother's Italian."

"Oh," she says, "I thought you were going to say that you were black or something..." and then she looks up, wide-eyed and apologetic. "Not that there's anything wrong with being black!"

Her reaction gets a good laugh out of me, and her face slightly reddens in response. "Actually," I say, "There's a little bit of that in there, too. My grandfather was black; my father is bi-racial."

"So, would you say you identify as that?" she asks, and I can see that she's not trying to be anything but curious.

"I mean, I'm not going out of my way to tell people that my grandfather was black, I respond. "I mainly identify as Italian because that's what I get from my mother. It's just another part of what makes you who you are right? Where you look like you're from, and who you were named after? I mean, it's always cool getting to tell people I was named after Hendrix, I say, taking a sip of my beer.

I glance over at her and I can see that she is wearing a blank expression on her face.

"Hendrix, I repeat, "You know...

She shrugs her shoulders.

"Jimi Hendrix? Electric Lady Land? Purple Haze?

"It's not ringing any bells, sorry.

"Seriously? I ask. "What about All Along the Watch Tower?

"Nope.

"Man, you *know* Jimi Hendrix. You just don't *know* that you know Jimi Hendrix, I tell her, and then I sing a few bars to her, desperate for a hint of recognition, before the whole night gets ruined. *"Let me stand next to your fire...*

"Oh! I know that one! she exclaims, "My dad used to listen to that song all the time.

"Your old man's got some taste, I say, with an air of exasperation. "If you don't know Jimi Hendrix by name though, he might've slipped up on his fatherhood game.

"It's not all his fault, she protests, pretending to be wounded. "I was too busy obsessing over boy bands and listening to Justin Timberlake.

"Ain't nothing wrong with my man JT, I concede, and she flashes me another smile made up of perfect teeth. "He's got cross-over appeal, and he's funny as hell when you see him on TV. I don't know if he can trump Jimi Hendrix, though.

"Is that what you and your dad used to listen to? she asks, and I know it's innocent small talk, but I roll deep with it anyway. I could lie if I wanted to, and sometimes I do when the subject comes up, but tonight feels like the truth might be the best bet, for the time being.

"You might say that," I answer. "My father wasn't around when I grew up, but he left behind a turn-table and a decent vinyl collection. So, in a roundabout way, yeah, that's what we both listened to."

"Sorry," she says quietly, and I can see she's slightly embarrassed.

"Don't be," I say, and I drain the rest of my beer in one quick gulp. "I mean, it really is a very decent vinyl collection." Then, as an afterthought, I add, "...even though it doesn't have any Justin Timberlake."

She laughs, and we both share a mutual feeling of gladness that things didn't just take a turn for the weird or awkward. "So do you collect old records like one of those hipster guys?"

"I don't know about hipster," I reply, "but you could call it a hobby."

"So your hobbies include pretending to be a criminal, collecting records, and picking up women at bars."

"You got me on the first two, but I wouldn't say I make a hobby out of picking up women in general. Just you."

"Smooth!" she exclaims with a broad laugh, and I smile back at her.

"Was it?" I ask in mock-sincerity. "I wasn't trying to be."

"Well you better start trying!" she says with wide eyes. "Otherwise this night is going to end badly for both of us!"

"Yes, ma'am," I respond, and I direct my attention to the server behind the bar. "*Dos cervesas, por favor!*"

She gives me a sardonic look after my order. "No wonder you get confused for being Spanish."

"When in Rome, do as the Romans do," I reply. "When at a Mexican joint, order like you know what you're doing. Besides, three years of Spanish in high school has to be good for something.

"So then if you actually know Spanish, do you ever try to pretend that that's what you are?

The question throws me off. I've pretended to be lots of things, usually without shame, but I don't think I've ever been outright confronted, however casually the question may have been asked.

"Sure, I answer, sticking to a broad form of the truth. "None of it's real, anyway, right? They teach you in college that race and culture are all social constructs, which to me means that if it's not biological, then it's all made up. If I can pass for white, black, Spanish, or Asian, why not go for it? I'm not hurting anybody; I'm just being multi-cultural.

"Multi-cultural? she asks as the next round of drinks gets placed in front of us.

"You like that? I ask with a grin as we reach over to our bottles. She smiles back at me as she takes her first sip.

"It was an impressive speech, she replies.

All signs are pointing to two consenting adults having sex in a few hours. This is where a lot of people, mainly guys, can screw up a sure thing. See, I'm not picky about where the night ends, but she strikes me as the type that does. She's been pretty overt with her signals. Is this feminism? She's certainly not being shy, which is fine by me, because I've never been too good with handling *shy*, myself. There's too great a chance for coming on too strong; too great a chance for miscommunication and hurt feelings. When you come across a woman with a healthy sexual appetite, you take things back to her place. I read it as a control thing. A woman goes to some strange guy's house and there might be too many unknown factors and variables. If you go to her place, she has the comfort of being on her home territory, and comfort is everything when you're prepping yourself to engage in a night of casual sex. Could it eventually be something more than casual? Sure, but I've never bothered to ask that question until the morning after.

I take a long pull from my drink, swallow hard, and lock

eyes with her. “All right,” I say, and I’m ready to go for broke. “I feel like it’s only fair to say that I’m into you, that I’m definitely into your birthmark, and I’m pretty sure you’re into all of my hobbies. Do you want to finish this round and go back to your place?”

Her eyebrows arch and she has a look that makes me think I may have just overplayed my hand and lost everything, but then she smiles and says, “Wow. Just like that?”

“Well, I was going to make up a story about how the heat’s gone out at my place, and then drop a terrible line about needing to find a way to keep warm tonight, but I thought you’d see right through that.”

“You’re right, I would have,” she says with a smile, and it’s only now just occurring to me how much alcohol I can smell on her breath. It’s making me wonder how much can be smelled on mine.

“So what do you think?” I ask, trying to push past the oddly lucid moment. If it’s going to happen, it needs to happen soon, so that we can both safely pass out satisfied afterwards, before either one of us turns sloppy and insufferable with all the booze we’ve been sucking back. Hooking up is an honest-to-God tightrope walk.

She looks at me hard for a moment, almost like she’s trying to look through me, and then her face breaks out into a very giddy, youthful smile.

“I’ve got a running tab,” I say to her with confidence. “We could leave right now...”

She doesn’t even wait for me to finish this statement before she picks up her nearly-full bottle and proceeds to drain it in what I find to be a crazy-sexy three seconds. She then grabs me by the wrist and leads me off of my stool and out of the bar to the nearest idling taxi.

This is not my first cab-ride with a perfect stranger on a Friday night, but this moment has always tricked me into feeling the excitement of something new and undiscovered. It’s the myth of promiscuity – that there is always some new and bold experience that is just waiting to be had, even though nothing is new or bold after your first time. You'd think that I'd know this by now, but in all of the taxis I've gotten into, up to and including this one, I don't think I've learned a damn thing about seemingly anything.

Two: Drop Off

Next mornings are awkward by design, and it's easy to see why. For most people dabbling in the practice of promiscuity, the morning after comes with a cloud of moral righteousness and the opinions of others that just sort of hangs over a pair of naked bodies, and whoever wakes up first gets to be the lucky one to get a jumpstart on wondering whether or not they've made a mistake, especially if they're concerned that someone may have gotten creative with their phone in the middle of the action, taking some very candid pictures. I'll bet people really miss the days of when a one-night stand used to be a secret between two people, and an easily dismissed rumor to anyone else. Now that we have smart phones and websites to broadcast everything, secrets and sex have a harder time co-existing.

I've been featured on a few social networks, and I guess maybe I felt a little bit of shame early on, like when it happened in high school, but I've had a few more years under my belt since then. A short stint in college happened, and my sense of shame grew a thicker skin over the span of those two years. It takes a whole lot more to get to me than it used to. Take my current situation as an example and you'll see what I mean.

There are a bunch of reasons why I should be ashamed right now. For starters, I can't remember half of the sex from last night, although I should've known that this would happen. At some point, I think we both started to feel a tidal wave of alcohol rushing through our blood streams, and by the time those waves made impact, she was using a card to quick pay for the cab ride. We were clumsily stumbling through her living room apartment, making our way toward what we hoped was her bedroom and not her roommate's, as I do believe we had decided entirely to forego the part where we turn on any lights. After that, I can only recall blurry fragments of moments that may or may not be imagined.

Science calls it *Alcohol-Induced Amnesia,* but everyone else calls it getting brown-out drunk; it's not all gone, but there aren't enough pieces left over to put a full picture together, and the impaired memory this morning has become the biggest source of what little shame I'm capable of. Try as I may, I cannot recall for the life of me what this woman's name is, nor can I remember the moment that I asked for it back at the bar. Of course, I could work to placate that sense of guilt by imagining that she's probably forgotten my name as well, but I do remember explaining to her that I was named after a rock and roll legend. No one ever forgets your name is Jimi when you explain its origin.

These are the moments when I have to become an amateur private investigator. She's sleeping soundly, so I very gently roll to my right and swing my legs over the bed. My feet hit a small pile of laundry, and a blurred memory of the two of us stripping each other down on this side of the bed resurfaces slightly before being pushed back by a small wave of nausea. I take one deep breath and double over to fish for my pants. Blood rushes to my temples and I swear I can hear my pulse beating inside of my ear drums. I've mistakenly grabbed her pants first, evident by the small waist and pink sequined phone sticking out of the pocket, which goes noted. A second trip brings up another wave of nausea and *my* pants, which mercifully still have my phone in the pockets as well. Score one for two consenting adults trying to use some discretion.

Whenever I'm in the situation of being the first one to wake up at a stranger's house, I have a small list of things that I typically must find, preferably before anyone else wakes up. Today's list includes:

1. ~~My pants~~
2. A bathroom
3. A source of water
4. Aspirin, ibuprofen, or some other derivative
5. A piece of mail with this woman's name on it

With my pants and my feet somewhat firmly on the ground, the next three things on the list are easy to find, mainly because they're all within close proximity of each other. This is the type of morning where I am grateful for medicine cabinets that have been well stocked, existing above sinks with cold running water that I can run my mouth under for days to swallow pills and drink enough to reassure my organs that I haven't given up on them.

After a quick search in the living room, I can see it's going to be a challenge to put the name to the face. I'm lucky enough to find a small basket containing mail, but unlucky in that there are envelopes featuring two different names. It's the curse of sleeping with a woman who has a female roommate, and you're the asshole who couldn't lockdown what her name was in the first place. Now I've got to risk it, and take the 50/50 odds. Speaking from experience, it's not fun when you lose that bet, either.

One letter has the name *Caitlin O'Meara* and the other says *Amanda Kavanagh*. Both of those names sound pretty damned Irish, and all I had going for me was the context of her looking Irish as hell...

"Jimi?"

Her voice calls out from the bedroom, and it sounds like mornings aren't too good to her. It lacks the same bounce and musical quality from the night before, but that usually comes with the territory of nursing a hangover, as I'm sure she is. I can make her morning even worse by being the guy who calls her by the wrong name. *Amanda* or *Caitlin*? I close my eyes and go for the one that sounds more Irish to me, with confidence:

"Good morning, Caitlin!"

"Ugh," she says, and I can feel myself tensing up, waiting for some kind of axe to fall that will make the morning worse for both of us. "I thought I told you to just call me *Cait*? Only my parents call me *Caitlin*."

The phones stayed in the pants *and* I got her name right? That's two wins in one morning. If I get any luckier, I'll drive over to the casino behind the stadiums and see where it takes me.

"Sorry, I tell her, "but you'll forgive me if my memory of last night is a little hazy.

"Tell me about it, she replies, and then asks, "Where are you right now?

"I'm in the living room, and then after a pause, I add in an apologetic tone, "I hope you don't mind, but I helped myself to your medicine cabinet.

"Oh my god, I know right? she calls back, and there's a bit of a whine in her voice. "My head is killing me! I don't think I'm ever going to drink like that again.

"I've heard that before, I say with a laugh, and I immediately regret it, because laughing makes my head hurt, and I can't help but wince. The thought occurs to me to drink more water, and then she says something that sobers me up entirely.

"Well, since you already know your way around the apartment, do you think you could grab me a few of those aspirins you found in the bathroom and pour me a glass of something to go with it?

I can't explain the surreality of the moment, but with this one simple request, I can see some dystopian future in which I have settled down with this *Caitlin* woman, who doesn't even really know who Jimi Hendrix is, and she is asking me to grab her pills, because we are an item and that is what is expected of me. Then, all of the other trappings of being with a person come pouring over me, and I quickly realize that I don't want to build a life with this person. *I should've called her the wrong name. I should've infuriated her and gotten her to kick me out of the apartment before it was too late, before she could ever have the chance to ask me to move in with her. I need to hit the self-destruct button immediately, before I'm trapped here forever...*

"Sure thing, I reply very coolly, and I waltz back into the bathroom, grab a couple of pills, and make a quick stop back into the kitchen to get her a bottle of water from the refrigerator before I make my way back into the bedroom, like I am the kindest and most genteel man you could ever hope to have a one-night stand with.

"These are for you," I say as I slip the pills into her hand and place the bottle of water on the night stand next to her bed. "I'm sorry you're not feeling well." I've sat down next to her on the bed when I say this last part so that I can reach down for my socks and shoes, and I guess she finds the sentiment sweet. She traces a finger along the spine of my shirtless back, and I can feel my eyes close at the presumption of this move. I can *feel* her thinking that we could be lovers, and I wish that she wouldn't. I feel sorry for her, knowing that I've already got one foot out the door, and I realize that I'm a bastard for always letting it come down to the morning after, and never the night of. I'd be stating my intentions a lot more clearly if I consistently left immediately after the sex was over, but I've never been able to deny myself the sense of satisfaction of sleeping next to someone who's just been satisfied. It's like a pat on the back for a job well done.

Now there's confusion. I stayed the night, and she probably thinks it means something. If I think about it for too long, *I* might start to think that it means something. The question "*What if she's the one?*" sometimes crops up in my mind in these situations, and without warning, here I am mulling over that very question as I lace up my sneakers. What if I'm just being a coward? What if I spend more time to get to know her and realize she's just my type? What if she's the one I want to introduce to my mother?

When I get confronted by a lot of these "What-ifs", I use a terribly arbitrary method I invented for discerning the difference between a one-night stand and a woman worth having a relationship with. Admittedly, the deck is stacked against the woman. In the few instances when I've used this method, the women failed miserably, and I've never heard from them again, which is typically the outcome I'm after. If a woman ever passes the Breakfast Test, that will be cause for consideration.

Now, I know what you're thinking. You're wondering if it's bullshit to "test" women in this fashion, and to that I say absolutely not. People test each other all the time; they test their strength, their loyalty, and sometimes even their intelligence. Everyone has some kind of a test they've developed that they employ on a need-to-know basis. I just happen to put a fancy spin on mine.

I could stop to explain the concept of the Breakfast Test, but it's simpler to let things play out naturally.

"You know what's a good cure for a hangover? I ask, and I turn to look at her as I finish tying the knots on my shoes. She pulls the sheet up to her chin and rolls onto her stomach, which is a classic morning-after maneuver. Her chest gets hidden by the bedding, but the sheet shifts over and exposes the whole of her back, which to her credit looks like a flawless stretch of porcelain, the kind that makes me want to lay against it, if for no other reason than to enjoy the contrast between her skin tone and mine. This is one of those inexplicable turn-ons that gets my blood going, and it's nearly a distraction. If you couple that with the way her hair is looking, all wild and untamed, we might not ever make it to breakfast. Mercifully however, she responds, and the sound of her misery indicates that she probably has zero interest in sex at the moment.

"Please don't say more alcohol, she groans, and she puts a hand up to her temple that elicits an immediate sense of empathy; both of us are battling some demons in a bottle this morning.

"What, you're not a fan of 'Hair of the Dog'? I ask her with a grin, and I can see her grimace at the thought of it.

"I'm not a fan of tomato juice, or any other substance that could be a color match for my hair.

I laugh aloud at this, and I take note of her sense of humor. If she was funny last night, I can't remember, and even if I could, it wouldn't count. Anyone can be funny when they're drunk, intentionally or no. A sober sense of humor should never be discredited, however. A fleeting thought passes through my mind that maybe I shouldn't worry about tests and the future; that I should explore and let things happen organically, but there is something in me that tends to drown out the instances of light-hearted fancy. It's the same something that's never allowed me to develop any meaningful adult relationships.

"Do you like orange juice?" I ask her, and I can see a look start to form over her face. Maybe she thinks I'm going to suggest something borderline-romantic; she looks intrigued.

"Yeah," she replies a bit apprehensively, "I suppose I could go for a glass of orange juice – just as long as you promise not to put any gin in it."

"No gin, I promise. I know a place that has some great fresh-squeezed juice and a solid breakfast menu. A big breakfast with some OJ can knock out any hangover. My treat."

"Well, if you're buying," she says. "Do they have pastries?"

"If you like Guava, this joint has a Guava pastry that's like nothing you've ever had before."

"Oh my god, *yes,* that sounds so exotic! Just let me grab a quick shower..."

She rolls back onto her side, but makes sure that she has the sheets in hand to keep herself covered. "You don't mind hanging out in the living room, do you?" she asks.

"Not at all," I say, and I pull out my phone with a little wave. "It'll give me a chance to catch up on some emails."

She smiles gratefully at me, probably because I didn't try to pull anything trashy and make it awkward by asking if she wanted any company. "I won't be long, I promise," she says.

"Take your time," I tell her, and I let myself out of the room, with my eyes set on my phone. It doesn't bother me when someone you had sex with the night before turns demure the next morning. That just means that the liquid courage has worn off. Besides that, who doesn't act a little differently when it's no longer night time and the sunlight starts to peak through the curtains of your bedroom windows? I can't be bothered by that.

What does bother me, however is the difference in understanding of what the phrase *I won't be long* means to various people. For instance, when I say this phrase, I'm basically asking you for ten or fifteen minutes. In my opinion, this should be the standard.

In the twenty-five minutes since leaving the room, I have responded to half a dozen emails and checked three different social media accounts. At last check, I was told that she needed five more minutes, which was six minutes ago.

"How we doing? I ask her, and I can hear the slight edge in her response.

"Almost ready, she replies, "Just give me thirty seconds.

Is this what it will be like if things are allowed to progress? Will this couch eventually have a worn out spot from my sitting and waiting for her to get ready for various events and activities? How much of my life will be spent just waiting to leave?

She steps into the living room and looks obnoxiously gorgeous. A bar or some nightclub I can understand getting primped for, but I have a short-list of about four or five diners that I like to take girls to, depending on where we are in the city, and all of them make their wages catering to the elderly and the sweat-pants crowd.

"You look too good, girl, I tell her, and she has no idea just how literal I'm being, smiling at the compliment.

We walk out of her building, and I get the chance to catch my bearings. I see the street signs and some of the familiar landmarks. Bits and pieces from the night before start to come together, and I recall wondering why we didn't just walk to her place from our drinking spot outside of Fells Point.

"Have you always lived in Butcher's Hill? I ask her.

"Nope, she says, and she shades her eyes against the morning sun. "I grew up in Jersey, but I moved down here for school. I'm actually in the process of finishing up my graduate degree at Hopkins. I've only got two months left! and she says this last part with an excited smile.

Suddenly, I don't feel bad about any tests at all.

I tell her I know a place that's very close by, and we continue to make small talk as we walk the four blocks up and two over to a little place called *Che's Diner*. It's a nice place to go to, if you don't mind ethnicity. The wait staff and a lot of the regular customers speak fluent Spanish with each other, and I guess that's why I've rarely ever seen any white people here. Sure, you might see the occasional walk-in, but if you don't speak Spanish, you get treated to a very thick accent and some badly broken English. It makes some people uncomfortable.

When I was a kid, my mother used to take me to places like this all the time, and I remember seeing two Spanish kids looking at me, and whispering to each other in their language. I leaned in on my mother, and said, "Mom, I think those kids are talking about me."

She didn't even look up from her plate, but just told me plainly, "That's because they are, Jimi."

"How do you know?" I asked her.

"Because I can speak Italian, and it's close enough to Spanish that I can figure it out," she said.

"Well, what are they saying?" I asked.

"Learn how to speak the language and you'll find out," she answered, and that was all that was said. If I think about it, I can still remember the paranoia I felt, not being able to understand what someone else was saying, wondering if they were talking about me, and how that drove me to study Spanish in school. I think that's the paranoia a lot of people feel when they're confronted by something that's foreign to them. The funny thing is, when I ask all of my white friends about what language they took in high school, a lot of them tell me they took French or German. I even knew one dude that took *Japanese*. Not enough people bother to learn Spanish, though, and because of that, most stay away from places like *Che's Diner*, for the most part.

"Oh my god, I can't believe I've never been in here before!" Caitlin says as we walk through the doors. She can't stop staring at the miniature palm trees in the corners of the room. "It's so *festive*!" she adds.

"Yeah, it's a pretty chill spot, I say, and I hold up two fingers to the waiter to indicate the number to be seated. He's a young guy, with dark hair slicked straight back, and a light mustache covering his upper lip. His dark skin stands out in stark contrast to his bright white t-shirt, and his slim build looks even more-so with the way his apron cinches in at his waist. Basically, he looks like a Spanish toothpick.

When we walk over to the table, he gives Caitlin a very friendly smile, but the look he gives me is a little more familiar, and it's almost a look of disapproval. It occurs to me that he's seen me before.

"Your waiter will be with you in a moment, he says, and to my surprise, there's no trace of an accent anywhere. As he walks away from the table, Caitlin reads the look on my face.

"What's the matter? she asks.

"Nothing, I say, "I just thought it was a rule that if you were going to work here, you had to be fresh off the boat.

"You're probably just upset that you won't get a chance to show off some more of your linguistic skills.

"Please, I tell her, "I don't need an invitation to flex knowledge, and I slap the table very hard before announcing in a voice loud enough for the whole diner to hear, "Dos café con leche, por favor!

Her shoulders tense up and she erupts in a nervous giggle as she immediately looks around the room to gauge the reaction of the other patrons. It's a slow morning, though, and the only other customers in the diner are a few scattered elderly people, chewing their breakfast and scrutinizing whatever's in front of them; newspapers, menus, or the television displaying some morning political talk show. The only people to take notice are a couple of waiters and a bus boy, and in two minutes we each have a steaming cup of hot, milky espresso in front of us.

"Wow, she says, looking at the cup in front of her. "Should I bother looking at the menu, or are you going to order for me?

"You do you, I say. "Get yourself a glass of that orange juice I was telling you about, if you want it. You just can't come to Che's and not have the coffee.”

“That's fair,” she replies, and begins to look over the menu.

“I thought you were all about that pastry?” I ask her.

“I *was*,” she says, “but then I saw the price.”

“It's a really big pastry, though,” I tell her.

“That's a bummer,” and she lets her bottom lip stick out a little bit in the same mock pout from the night before. “I hate being a poor college student.”

“It's no sweat,” I say. “My treat. Get whatever you want.”

She smiles when I say this, and when the waiter comes over, she proceeds to order the Guava pastry, with a side of scrambled eggs, and bacon. For my own part, I order a bowl of fruit and tostada, and we go about our morning, making small talk while eating our breakfast. We talk about her studies, and I do my best to follow along, but she's getting a degree in biology, and I can't understand a damn thing about what it is that she actually does. My attempts to have her break it down for me don't help much, either, and the conversation wanes a bit, skewing more toward awkward silences accentuated by the sounds of our chewing. By the time I've gotten to the bottom of my fruit bowl, and her meal has dwindled down to just a couple of small bites, I figure it's just about that time.

“Stay put and enjoy the rest of your breakfast,” I tell her. “I'm just gonna swing by the men's room and grab the check.”

“Okay,” she says, smiling sweetly while picking at another bite of her food.

I walk away from the table and around the corner to the counter where the register is. Behind the counter is the waiter who seated us, and he's wearing the same look on his face when he sees me. I try not to take notice.

“You mind if I pay the bill real fast?” I ask him, and I hand him a twenty.

The waiter shakes his head slightly as he takes the money, and as his eyes fall to punching numbers on the cash register, I hear him mutter something under his breath.

"You say something? I ask him, and I lean in a little closer. He raises his eyes to me, and now it's plain to see that the waiter is wearing a sincere look of disgust, and he's not even remotely intimidated by my leaning in on him.

"This another *chica* you're gonna feed then leave?

Now I know why he doesn't like me, and I realize that I've pulled the Breakfast Test in this place once before. For whatever reason, it brings a smile to my face.

"Maybe, maybe not, I tell the waiter with a shrug of my shoulders, "It always depends on the *chica*. You can keep that change, by the way, I add, before leaving the counter. It's easy to walk away from a condescending stare-down when the person doing the staring doesn't know anything about you, and I'll be damned if some wait staff is ever going to make me feel a certain kind of way.

The trip to the bathroom is only so that I can quickly wash my hands of the sticky residue left by the mango and papaya, and to take a quick look in the mirror. You need a game face before you do something like this, and it's all in the eyes. I check my reflection, practice my look once or twice, and then leave to go back to the table.

When I approach her, she can see that there's something wrong.

"What is it? she asks me, and I shake my head as I sink down to my chair, looking like I want to kick myself.

"I'm so embarrassed, I say, with eyes cast downward. "I think I must've left my card back at the bar last night, and I don't have any cash on me.

"You're kidding, right? and she's still wearing the same smile from when I left for the bathroom. I bring my eyes up to meet hers, and I hold my practiced look. Slowly, I can see her own expression start to change.

"Is there any way you can pay the bill? I ask her.

"Are you *fucking* kidding me? she whispers, and I can see her starting to panic. “I literally have, like, fifty dollars to my name right now!”

“It was an honest mistake on my part,” I tell her, and I can see her panic start to turn to anger. “I seriously thought I still had my card on me.”

“But who *does* that?” she protests.

“Does *what*?” I ask, allowing myself to become a bit defensive.

“Who the fuck asks somebody out, says it’s their treat, and then doesn’t stop to check to see if they’ve got any money with them? It’s fucking *irresponsible*.”

This is when the switch gets flipped, and I can feel myself get cold to any feelings that could’ve been forming between the two of us.

“Don’t worry about it,” I tell her. “I was just fucking with you. Bill’s already paid.”

“Wait, what?” she asks, and the look on her face is totally bewildered.

“Yeah, it’s cool,” I tell her. “I paid the bill already. But go ahead and talk to me about being irresponsible when you’re bringing home dudes you hardly even know.”

My look is smug. The words cut into her, and it takes a second for her to realize where she is, who she’s with, and what she’s doing. When it all registers, she gives me a look that’s a mixture of anger, sadness, and humiliation. I can see that she’s fighting back tears. She gets up out of her chair so abruptly, that it falls backward. As it falls to the floor, it’s enough to alert what few people are in the diner that a scene is about to go down.

“You’re a fucking creep!” she says, and she picks up her café con leche, what’s left of it, and throws it in my face. It’s still warm, and it makes a good splash, but it’s not hot enough to burn. She slams the cup down on the table, turns away, and storms out of the diner. As she leaves, just about everyone can hear her muttering to herself.

“Why is every guy I meet such a complete asshole?”

I grab the end of the table cloth and wipe my face down

before getting up to leave. I want to give her a minute's head start so that we don't have to worry about running into each other again. As I get up to go, I cross the counter where the register is, and the one waiter is still behind it. I hear him whispering to another waiter as I pass, and I know that my childhood paranoia was at least somewhat justified.

"*...pendejo* he says, loudly enough for me to hear as I'm walking by.

I stop and turn to him, politely nod, and say, "*Gracias,* before walking out of the diner myself. There's not much else you can do in that situation, especially when there are worse things in the world than having warm coffee thrown in your face and a judgmental waiter cussing at you in Spanish. It's not my problem if they can't see that it's better this way. Caitlin will finish up school, leave the city and go back to Jersey, and I will be a distant memory. She has to realize that I'm not the guy you want to have a relationship with. I've never really seen a good one, so I wouldn't know how they function.

Three: Sundays

I don't sleep with random women every weekend, or even every *other* weekend, but I do sleep around enough to have some kind of reputation. Stories get around to other people, and if you're the guy at the center of five or six of these stories, and they are interesting enough to commit to memory, then that becomes who you are whether you like it or not. It's a lazy way to form an opinion of somebody, through hearsay, but what can you do about it?

There's always going to be more to me than what I'll typically let on, although there isn't a particular reason as to why I don't discuss some things. Maybe it's just because I'm better at collecting acquaintances than I am collecting friends. With acquaintances, you can talk about sports or music, and it's all good, but that's the limit. Only friends will let you talk about the deeper stuff, like politics, your messed up family, or your job.

Personally, I *hate* my job. It makes no use of the Associate's Degree that I earned spending two years at a community college. It can be pretty labor intensive, sometimes even dangerous, and I don't always work with the most trustworthy of people. The upshot, however, is that the pay is decent and allows me to maintain some kind of comfortable routine.

Fridays are for getting drunk.

Saturdays are for recovering.

Sundays are for visiting my mother.

Is it out of a sense of love or obligation that I do this every Sunday? I don't know that I can say, if I'm being honest. It's just something that's always been done as far back as I can remember.

I never knew my mother's parents. Both of them died around the time my mom was finishing her second year at the community school. Johnny Di Paola lost his life in a car accident at the age of 53, as he was coming home from his job at the chemical plant in the city. His wife, Deena, had experienced small chest pains while planning for her husband's funeral, but didn't tell anyone until they put her in a hospital bed the night before Johnny's funeral. She died the next day (extended family members would say of a broken heart), and Vivian Di Paola, an only-child, found herself without a mother or father in less than the span of a week. The closest I got to ever knowing them was from the select stories she used to tell me about when I was a kid, and they would make me smile. I bet Johnny and Deena would've been nice people to meet.

When Mom lost her parents, she sold their home and used the money to pay off the funeral expenses, medical bills, and any remaining debts, including what she owed for school. With the money left over, she crafted herself a small budget and used it to find an apartment that she could afford by herself. To my knowledge, Mom has always been an independent woman like that. She got a job as a laboratory technician at the local hospital, and she made the effort to put herself in a good spot. She was saving money, working full-time, and having the occasional bit of fun with some of the girlfriends she knew from work. Then she met my father.

I don't really know much about their history. I remember asking my mother once, when I was thirteen or fourteen, "How did Dad ask you out? I guess I was looking for something I could relate to, because I was getting to be that age. Instead, I just remember Mom looking at me and dropping a bomb.

"Jimi, she said, *"It's so embarrassing, I don't even know why I said 'yes'.*

That was the entire story that she gave me.

It was a cold response to give a kid, but it's not like she was that cold all the time; not on purpose, anyway. Growing up, my father wasn't ever around, but that didn't stop my mother from making sure that I "keep up with my people .

"Family is everything, Jimi, she'd say. *"You always keep up with your people, no matter what.*

And so here I am, keeping up with the only people I've got, every Sunday like clock-work.

Mom's place isn't the same as where I grew up. She'd kept the apartment that she had after her parents died right up to the point I graduated high school, and by that time, she had a mantra that she kept chanting over and over, all throughout my senior year. If we had a fight, she'd say it. If she got the mail and saw a load of bills, she'd say it. If she got a call to go in for work because someone called out, she'd say it:

Life begins at forty.

She wasn't lying, either. The day I left for college was the day she left the apartment. She found a very small home in a town outside of the city; an ancient three-bed, one-bath duplex that needed some serious rehab work. While I was turning nineteen and getting my general education requirements knocked out in my first year of school, Mom was turning forty, studying internet videos on how to safely take out a wall with a sledgehammer, and how to hang new dry-wall in its place. She still had some of the same girlfriends at work from before I was born, and they'd all get together in hard hats and work clothes, open a bottle of wine, and literally tear a room apart. It must've been cathartic for them, and they only ever had one rule: No men allowed.

When I walk into the house, there's always something new to admire, or comment on. New smells interchange and hang in the air, whether it's the scent of old plaster walls that have been torn down, or fresh coats of paint that have been applied to the new walls in their place. Today, it's the flooring.

"What happened to the carpet, Mom? I ask her, and I see her peek her head out of the kitchen doorway.

"Do you like it? she asks, examining the new hardwood floors as if she's still trying to decide for herself. She takes a few steps into the living room, with her eyes on her handiwork, scanning up and down the seams of the flooring. "We went to one of those furniture liquidator places and got a bunch of this flooring for super cheap. It's already done for you with the staining and everything. You just have to snap it into place.

"So what? You just decided one day to rip out all of the

carpets in the place and put in hardwood floors on your own?

"Jimi, she says, in the same tone she has used with me since I was a boy for when she would have to repeat herself, "I've been complaining about the carpets in here for *years.* The vacuums they have out now don't do *shit* compared to the way they used to make them. I could never get the floors clean, and honestly, I was just sick and tired of it. How many times have I been telling you that?

The look on my face suggests I have no recollection of anything, and she rolls her eyes at me.

"Just compliment me on how nice the damn floors look and get inside, she tells me, and then adds as an afterthought, "and take your shoes off before you take one more step!

I step further inside and slip off my sneakers, and with a bright, artificial tone, I tell her, "The damn floors like real nice, Mom.

"Ha ha, she says, dryly. She has her back to me, walking toward the kitchen, and I can't help but notice how it always seems to be with her when I come around the house. She looks tired, as if she's just undergone some great deal of work and is ready to collapse. I try not to let it happen, but it bothers me deep down inside when I think about it, maybe because it's such a far cry from some of the pictures that I've seen her post online, lately.

With all of the home improvement projects, she started a "Do It Yourself blog. She said she wanted to show women her age that "anyone can get it done, just as long as they have the right kind of support. Mom's got her girlfriends, and they are her support. When she posts her projects online, I think she feels that she in turn is becoming somebody's best girlfriend from the internet – right up there with the daytime talk show hosts that people watch on television; the ones you'll never meet, but just know you'd feel right at home with if they were to show up on your doorstep one day to visit over coffee.

She updates the blog sporadically, but each update is incredibly detailed. Every project warrants a new post, and she talks about what she's doing, why she's doing it, how much *they* say it's going to cost, how much of that cost is a rip-off, and what it *really* can cost in the long-run, if you do it yourself. Her posts include before, during, and after pictures, and she posts them throughout the write-up of each project. When I look at these pictures of my mother, standing next to all of the friends who helped her in each project, and how happy she looks; how accomplished she looks, it burns me up a little inside. I don't know a time that I've ever seen her have a face like that around me.

But then again, I'm also not featured in any of the pictures on her blog.

We've never had that type of relationship, though. If you were to ask me if I thought I was a good son to my mother, I'd tell you with confidence that I was and am. Outside of the one time in high school (which barely counts), I've never been arrested, and I *never* experimented with hardcore drugs. I finished college on time, and I'm not some post-grad asking her for money on a regular basis; I have not lived with her since moving out after high school, and the thought of moving back in with her has never been up for consideration. I call her on her birthday and I visit every Sunday, as well as come around on major holidays. On paper, I am today's perfect son. There are parents in this world that would *kill* to have me as their own.

Not my mother, though. We have a history. She just looks resigned to the fact that I am her son, and welcomes me into her home without great fanfare. This is how we engage with each other. Our actions are the product of routine more so than they are of love. I come to her house. She invites me in. We make small talk. I sometimes share a meal with her, and we sometimes watch a television show. The closest we get to love and affection is when I ask her about her health. She can be stubborn and doesn't like going to the doctor's office, and if she has some kind of an ailment it typically takes an argument between the two of us about why I think she needs to get something checked out before anything gets done. We'll go back and forth with each other, and I'll always end my point by telling her that I'm only getting on her because I love her and want her to hang around a little longer, which usually does the trick. I was able to convince her to tackle a bout of walking pneumonia and one worrisome lump in her wrist that ended up being a benign tumor with those arguments, which allowed me to feel like a dutiful son.

Other than those moments, I keep our visits short. If I stay for too long, a fight breaks out that *isn't* about her health, and I almost always end up leaving mad and embarrassed. It's typically about my job or my love life, and those can be some powerful arguments. It sometimes makes me wonder if my mother doesn't realize that they're just echoes of the same arguments she would have with my paternal grandmother.

My grandmother, of course, is the reason for there being a tradition of visiting on Sundays; it was my mother's desire that I keep up with my people. Unfortunately, my mother's parents were dead, and my father was in jail. The only people that I could keep up with were my *other* grandparents, Patrice and Yvette Mercier; my Pop-Pop and Yaya.

The memories of Pop-Pop are somewhat vague now. He died before I turned eight, and I can only recall brief impressions of a dark-skinned, big bellied man, who liked to sit in his recliner and watch baseball anytime we came over to visit.

"Come over here and sit next to your Pop-Pop, he'd say, and I'd sit on the arm of his chair, lean in on him, and watch the Orioles play. Sometimes he'd cuss about the pitching, and I would giggle at the curse words, because every time he'd let one slip, he'd stop what he was saying and whisper in my ear, "*Pop-Pop shouldn't have said that. Don't you go talking like that, Jimi. You're gonna be a good boy.*

When Pop-Pop was around, things were more than civil – they were absolutely peaceful. I don't think they ever thought it was ideal that their son was in jail, obviously, but I know that they loved my mother for coming around regularly to bring their only grandson around for regular visits. It made them happy, and took away some of the guilt. I'm almost positive that if Patrice Mercier had been able to have his way, he would've made up for his son Antoine's mistakes by raising me up himself. Some things just don't pan out the way you want them to, though.

Pop-Pop passed away in his chair in the middle of the night in the summer of 97. He told his wife he was going to stay up and watch the rest of the Orioles game – they were playing the Angels, and Mike Mussina was throwing a good game. The game was being played in Anaheim, however, and didn't start until after 10pm. Yvette, my Yaya, couldn't make it past 11 o'clock, and went to bed without her husband. When she woke up the next morning, Pop-Pop was still sitting in his chair, very still, and had gone cold for some time.

It was a hard time for everyone, and marked a real change in my Yaya, especially with the way that she regarded my mother and me. Before her husband's death, she used to watch from afar, marveling at how the two of us would interact with each other. Once he died, she stopped marveling from afar and became a lot closer. Yaya would smother me with hugs and kisses when I walked in the door, and if there was something that I wanted, Yaya would get it for me, regardless of how my mother felt.

And that was how things had changed between Yaya and my mother. When it came to the subject of Jimi Di Paola, neither woman could ever see eye to eye.

"Why don't that boy have his father's name?' Yaya would ask. It was a subject that was brought up every now and again after Pop-Pop died. The first few times it happened, Mom would try to gloss over the topic with various responses:

"You know why, Yvette.'

"We already talked about this, Yvette.'

"Antoine got his say with what Jimi's first name should be, Yvette.'

These responses would sometimes do the trick for a moment or two, but only provided a temporary peace. When the subject came up again, Yaya would get bolder and bolder still.

It started with birthday cards and Christmas cards. Yaya

would address the letters to "Jimi Mercier , which Mom took as a joke the first time, but by the third time was becoming angrier with each passing instance. The last straw, however, was when during one Sunday visit, Yaya passed Mom a couple of papers over the dinner table while they drank their coffee after breakfast.

Mom scanned over the pages, and when she looked up from them, her eyes took on a fiery quality, and Yaya's look was resolute in return.

"*What's this supposed to be?* my mother had asked.

"*Just some papers I found online,* Yaya had said, bringing her coffee to her lips, enforcing a degree of casualness over what she knew was a tense subject.

"*Papers on getting a name changed?*

"*If you look through the pages, you'll see it's easier to get done than you'd think, and I could take care of all of the costs.*

I remember quietly eating a powdered donut with a short glass of milk, going from look to look, like I was watching some intense tennis match play out. When my mother broke eye contact, it was to look at me:

"*Go wait in the car.*

Of course I didn't wait in the car. I was ten years old and old enough to understand that something was about to go down, and it could not be missed. I parked myself on the front porch step and barely breathed for fear that the sound of my breath would cause me to miss a moment of what was going to happen. When it started though, they were loud enough that I didn't miss a single syllable.

"*How many times, Yvette?*

"*You have no right to deny that boy his legacy, Vivian. You're wrong, and you know you're wrong.*

"*Wrong? You want to talk to me about wrong?*

"*Don't you throw that up there like you got the moral high ground!*

"*I don't pretend to have the moral high ground, Yvette. I know I have the moral high ground."*

"Jimi ought to have his father's name. It's not right this way. It's not natural.

"When are you going to understand? I AM HIS FATHER. I am his mother, AND I am his father. He's a Di Paola, because that's all he's GOT in this world.

This conversation is burned into my brain. I couldn't explain today all of the feelings I was experiencing then, but I remember crying when my mother said that, and after that, the front door bursting open.

"Jimi Andrew Di Paola, I thought I told you to get your ass in the car!

I bolted from the front step and sprinted to the back seat of my mom's ride. Yaya followed close on my mother's heels. She looked flustered, angry, but wasn't crying like my mother and me.

"So you're just gonna pack Jimi up and leave me to be by myself? You made a promise to me!

My mother, in the middle of a powerful stride, found it within herself to stop on a dime and turn to face Yaya.

"Yvette, I am sorry about your husband, she said, *"and I miss him just as much as you do. I would've done anything to see Patrice be a bigger part of Jimi's life, but Patrice isn't Antoine, and you're not helping things. I promised you every Sunday, and I will keep that promise, but there are boundaries, Yvette, and you have got to stop crossing them.*

That night ended by being the first time I ever saw my mother fix herself a drink. True to her word, however, we visited Yaya every Sunday, and the subject of my name was never brought up again. Yaya found other boundaries to push, though.

Some visits were calm and polite, but those are the visits that I have the most trouble remembering. I can only vividly remember the visits that were turbulent, marred by tension and unresolved conflicts, and I was at the center of every argument. I might be doing something stupid or dangerous, and my mom would fuss at me; or I'd be playing a videogame instead of doing the dishes that I was asked to take care of after dinner, and Mom would snap. It didn't matter the situation – Yaya was always on my side.

"*You stop fussing at the boy in my house,* she'd always say. If my mom tried to protest, she'd get the same pushback, every single time:

"*You yell at him too much. He's just a baby.*

This went on for years, I think. I'm not sure, because it's hard to remember the fights themselves. What I do know is that after Pop-Pop died and the fight over my last name happened, Mom started drinking more. It started off as something that was occasional; some Sunday nights, depending on how stressful Yaya had been. After a while though, Sunday night went into Monday night, and eventually Mom turned into an evening drunk.

When you're a kid, you don't think it's that bad. There was always plenty of booze to lift, and I was able to get myself and a couple of buddies drunk for the first time when we were only in the 8th grade. The way I figured, if I got my kicks in while my mother's got hers, everything was copacetic. If you had asked me then, I would've told you that the only way the arrangement could've been any better was if Mom and I were getting drunk together.

My first time drinking led to very social Freshman and Sophomore years of high school. We never had the party at my place, because it was too small, but I could always be relied upon to bring a bottle to someone else's house, and I quickly made friends with the older kids. My grades might have looked like shit, but none of that mattered, because I didn't have a parent looking over my shoulder. It was a lifestyle; a drunk and her son living separate lives under the same roof.

And then one day, everything changed. Quickly.

Yaya started having heart problems around the same time I began high school. By the end of my first year, she was diagnosed with congestive heart failure. She held on for as long as she could, but passed away a little over a year later, right before I was set to start Junior year of school. When we went to the funeral, my mother had herself what an alcoholic refers to as *a moment of clarity.* Right up to this moment, she didn't see any problems with her life. She went to work, got paid, took care of the bills, and kept me fed with a roof over my head. As far as she was concerned, that was the job, and she was going above and beyond by keeping her promise to Yaya, bringing me around every Sunday for family visits. She didn't have friends that she went out with at all hours of the night, and she certainly didn't sleep around. She drank alone, in her home, usually with a book in hand or a television on; an army of one, plus a son. Maybe she thought she was keeping a lid on it that way, but it never stopped my Yaya from finding things out. We'd spend time together, and Yaya would pry, though I never knew that that's what it was. She'd ask about my mother and I wouldn't hesitate to mention her drinking, because I wasn't aware that there was anything wrong with it, and Yaya would get all of her information from me through a line of casual questions. It never occurred to either one of us that my Yaya talked about my mother to her friends; her grand-baby Jimi, sure, but not *her.* They didn't even like each other, so why talk about each other to other people?

The funeral was an eye opener. My mother could feel the heat from a dozen set of eyes, and I could, too. It was hard not to notice, and for the first time in my life, I felt embarrassed by what had become of my mother. I could hear people whispering, and once I was able to make out someone saying, *"I'll bet she makes a fool of herself at the wake. You know they've got an open bar.*

We never talked about it, but I know my mother must've heard those very same things, too, because they *did* have an open-bar, but she never once got up to visit it. She just sat at our table, stone-faced while strangers came up to offer us their condolences, sipping on a Styrofoam cup of black coffee. When we left the wake and got home, she grabbed every bottle of alcohol we had, dumped it down the kitchen sink, and then threw the bottles into the trash can hard enough that they shattered, every single one of them. When she finished with that, she went into her bedroom, locked the door, and cried until she fell asleep. She never spoke a word to me about it after that; she didn't make any bold proclamations about turning over a new leaf, offer any flowery apologies about the past, or even attend any group meetings. It just went understood that Yaya's funeral marked the first day of her sobriety. Things were going to change, and they did. If my mother wasn't going to spend her evenings drinking, she was going to spend them being an invested parent, whether I liked it or not.

It started with an off-hand comment, maybe a week before school was set to start. *"Jimi-boy,* she'd said, *"we're gonna have to do something about these grades this year.* At that point, I hadn't yet believed that sobriety was going to stick, so it didn't bother me. I rolled my eyes to it, maybe said something like, *"Yeah, sure thing, Ma.* I can't remember for certain, but I do know that I had no idea what was coming next.

The school year began; I went to my classes, mainly to see my friends and find out what was happening later. I sometimes screwed with my teachers, just so I could get a rise out of the other idiots I sat near; consequences had not been a thing for me, so I acted that way just because. It didn't occur to me that my mother would start asking me to answer for my actions, and when she did, I still couldn't take her seriously.

She'd say, *"You're grounded.*

I'd say, *"Okay,* knowing full well she couldn't keep me in the house.

And then one night, I tested it. I went to go walk out the door, and she asked me, *"Where the hell do you think you're going?*

I said, *"I'm going to Joe's place.*

"Who's Joe?

"A guy from school. He's having a party."

"Aren't you forgetting something?"

"No. What?"

"You're grounded!"

The look I gave her was the kind that every parent wants to

slap off of their kid's face, even the ones that have never lifted a finger toward their child. I turned to leave, and a voice erupted deep from within my mother, like some sort of primal growl.

"Don't you dare walk out of this apartment."

"*Watch me,*" I said, and I thought I was so cool about it that I didn't even slam the door behind me. I went to Joe's, a guy who I didn't have any classes with and never even met, made a beeline for his cooler, and shot-gunned the first can of beer I could get my hand around. A small crowd gathered to watch me murder the drink, and there was a smattering of applause when I crushed the can on my forehead. I thanked my audience and told them that for my next trick, I was going to get fucked up. They laughed, and I got right to work on catching a buzz. Twenty minutes later, the cops showed up.

People scrambled for their cars, but three police vehicles put a stop to anyone leaving. They had us lined up against the wall in the backyard; fourteen high school students of varying age, while a cop made Joe (whom I still had not been officially introduced to) open and dump out each can of beer from the two thirty-packs he had stolen from his father (who was leaving early from his night-shift, presumably to kick his son's ass).

I should've known something was up when an officer was going down the line, eying each one of us. When he got to me, he gave me a hard look, and then asked me, "Are you Jimi Di Paola?" I swallowed hard, told him I was, and the officer looked over his shoulder and said to another cop, "This is the one." I was promptly spun around and read my rights while being cuffed. Everyone else was forced to call a parent to come and pick them up from the property; I was put in the back of a police cruiser and made to spend the night in a holding cell.

My mother came to pick me up the next morning, and she brought with her a change of clothes; a sausage, egg, and cheese biscuit; a hot cup of coffee, and my backpack for school. I didn't say a word to her. I grabbed the biscuit and threw it in the trash can, and dropped the coffee in behind it. I took the clothes, got changed in the bathroom, and walked out of the precinct with her in total silence.

To her credit, Mom didn't flinch at any single thing I did that morning. She kept her ground and let the quietness of the moment happen, right up to the point where she pulled up to the front of the school. I stared ahead, gnashing my teeth in anger, choking back the humiliation, but Mom was resolute. She had put the automatic locks on the door, so there was no way of leaving before she could have her say.

I expected yelling and screaming, but was thunderstruck by the serenity in her voice.

"Jimi," she said, "If you want to be like your father, keep doing what you're doing. I just won't pick you up next time. If you don't want to be like your father, then you had better do as I say, and get your work done at school. The choice is yours, son," and she punctuated the statement by popping the unlock button on the car. Her words stung on multiple fronts, and I didn't want to give her the satisfaction of a response. I left the car, still mute, and walked into the building.

A fire raged in me that year. I found myself hating everyone who was at that party, and all of their friends, by proxy. It was pretty easy to cut out my social life; because I was the only one that was hand-cuffed, everyone assumed it was my mother that had called the cops, and my name was mud as a result. A few people even tried to pick a fight with me, especially Joe, whom I still did not know nor cared enough about to be bother by the fact that he had to deal with a raft of shit from his father, who was naturally upset about cops having to raid his house. I just didn't participate in any of it; I was filled with a new drive and determination – to graduate and get out.

I did not say a word to my mother for two weeks, but eventually I softened. She never pushed, never screamed or hollered, and only told me enough to know that she was keeping tabs on me. Time went by, and our relationship transformed into a grudging sort of respect; it didn't feel like love, but I came to understood what she did for me, and I think she understood (or at least *tolerated*) the direction I took. She didn't fight me on my decision to skip my high school graduation, and I accepted her offer to celebrate with a quiet dinner at a nice restaurant. I did two years of community college, and paid what I could. Mom paid the rest, and I ended with an Associate's Degree in Business Administration, of all things.

When I left home for good, I made the decision to visit every Sunday, and with the exception of one or two instances of being sick or away, I've kept my visits constant. Today's visit is the same as it ever was. After complimenting the floors of her house, I walk into her kitchen and we sit together, sipping cups of coffee. Conversation is sporadic through our first two cups, and only picks up when she goes to the cabinet and grabs a box of cookies before throwing them onto the table.

"Eat these," she says, "before they go stale."

I look at the box, and I see that they're the ginger snaps that Yaya used to buy me when I was a kid.

"Wow," I say. "What's up with the throw-back?"

Mom stares at the box thoughtfully. "I don't know," she replies. "I saw them sitting on the shelf a couple of weeks ago. They were on sale. I just grabbed them. Forgot how sweet they were, though."

I pull one of the ginger snaps out of the box; a small, sugar-frosted brown cookie, and I can feel that it's already gone a little soft. Still, I dip it in my coffee and take a bite. Mom's right about the sweetness, and it marries with the coffee's bitterness in a way that stops it from tasting like my childhood. I contemplate the flavor and look up at my mother.

"Yeah," I say to her, "these are pretty gross."

"You think so, too?" she asks. "Just go ahead and throw them out."

I get up, stretch my legs, toss the box of cookies in the garbage can, and place my coffee cup in the sink. I stand in the door way and turn to face my mother. She's seated back at the table, still sipping her coffee. She looks up at me and stares thoughtfully.

"Well, I say to her, "I think I'll just leave it at a cup of coffee, today. I'm going in at midnight to do inventory, so I'm just gonna go back to the home front and get to bed at a decent hour.

"Mmhmm, my mother replies, knowingly. "That third shift is a *bitch.*

"You know it, I reply, and I turn to walk out over her shiny new hardwood floors, when she calls out to me, right as I'm approaching the front door.

"Jimi? she calls out.

"Yeah, ma? I answer, with my hand on the door knob. There is a silent pause that hangs in the air.

"Never mind, she says. I have a vague understanding of what the question could be, and I get why she doesn't ask it. Why bother with questions when the answers don't change?

"See you next Sunday, I say to her.

"I'll see you then, she replies.

Four: Work

You can call me a lot of things. Lazy isn't one of them. If it looks like I party every once in a while, so be it. I'm working the rest of the time.

My typical schedule is five days a week. Really, it's supposed to be four ten-hour shifts, but there's always overtime where I work. Back-logs happen; people call-out sick, sick people come in and don't get anything done, lazy people come in and don't get anything done - there are all kinds of reasons you can collect overtime, and I collect regularly. Lately, the work's been good, and I've been hitting fifty hour work weeks for the past month and a half.

I'm a lumper and a picker, and the jobs are as glamorous as their title. Long haul trucks pull into the warehouse, and if I'm lumping, I unload the product with a partner, put it on pallets, and then seal it up with a giant roll of plastic wrap. If I'm picking, it means I'm grabbing up special pallet orders for local grocery stores, running around the warehouse like a madman with a checklist; I find the product, put it on the pallet, and get it ready for hauling, quick, fast, and in a hurry. Lumping is slower, because it pays by the hour, and if you work too fast, you work yourself out of a paycheck. Picking pays by the item, since backlogs can happen so quickly and they need incentive pay to get you to work fast. Either way, I'm good at what I do, because I like the paycheck. The job itself might suck, but it's work you don't have to think too hard about and it lets you be physical, and I do so enjoy a good workout.

When I walk into the warehouse, I'm equipped with the tools of the trade. The dock is like a giant freezer, and the whole place is kept at around 20 degrees, with the exception of the deep freeze units that are kept at Zero. You can't be unprepared for this sort of environment; the cold will never forgive you for it. New guys get it the worst, because the job attracts a certain kind of rough-neck who think they're tough as nails.

"You have to wear layers," you might tell them, and they'll

look at you like you're the biggest punk on the planet - like they know how to handle the cold and you're just a little bitch who can't hack it. Then three hours into their first night on the dock, they start moaning because they didn't listen when you told them about the wool socks, or at least wearing two pair if all you had was cotton; they don't realize that their steel-toe boots can be conductors of the cold, and that because they're not wearing a hat, they've got body-heat escaping from the tops of their skulls and their brains don't want to freeze to death, so heat starts being pulled from the body's expendable extremities, like the ears, the nose and fingertips, or the toes that are already butting up against frozen steel. The science behind those facts is as cold as the air inside the dock, and it can sting hard if you aren't prepared for it. The new guys that come unprepared and don't listen when you give them good advice are the guys that take a smoke break and never come back. They leave, go to the bar, and tell everyone what a miserable job it is being a lumper. Eventually the warehouse gets a reputation and it makes it harder to find people that will do the work. That's why I get stuck on shifts with people that suck at their job, but don't get fired because they don't mind the cold. That's why I get stuck on a shift with Harris Crockett.

I don't think anybody takes him seriously. He's the worst of the worst; a sycophantic wannabe hard ass who likes to boast about street cred he's never had. When people call him by his last name, they call him "Crock-of-Shit to his face and he acts like he's in on the joke, like he revels in the namesake, and it's disgusting. Some days his personality wears thin, and words can't describe how much I hate Harris Crockett on those days, but then other days he's all right and you know that he's better than some of the other alternatives that are getting hired and fired inside the warehouse. It all depends on the day, I guess, and that's my main issue with him. You just never know what kind of day it's going to be when you get paired up with Harris.

When I walk into the staff room to grab my time card, he's already sitting at one of the tables, leaning back in one chair with his boots propped up on another, and a warm coffee resting on the round of his belly.

"*Hound Dog,*" he yells at me when I punch in, like we're best friends and that I don't hate being called that name, "You ready to get this inventory done or what?"

"Harris," I reply, and I don't even bother with eye contact. "You're here awful early for someone who's not planning on doing a damn thing."

"Shit," he says, "the job pays by the hour, doesn't it? If I work too hard, I won't get paid!"

"We're picking," I say. "We get incentive pay."

"We do?" he asks, and the sound of his sarcasm makes me tense up.

"Just don't get in my way," I tell him, and I make my way back to the manager's office.

Buck Johnson is sitting behind his desk when I walk in, and when he looks up from his papers, he pushes his thick glasses up off the bridge of his nose and gives me a wide smile.

"There's my guy," he says to me, and his voice has a rasp to it that sounds like three decades of filtered 100s that have been smoked from one end to the other. The warehouse has been around for a long time, and at one point, he was one of those prime-movers; a stocky, barrel-chested hustler that moved product quickly and gave you an earful when you were slow. Now he's just a fat man on the other side of the desk, giving the orders instead of processing them, keeping count of the number of days he has left before he can collect his pension. When he sees me, though, he sees himself from back in the day, and I know when he calls me his "guy" that he's being genuine and not at all derogatory. Buck's always been alright in my book.

"What you got for me tonight?" I ask him, and he tosses a thick stack of orders fixed to a clip board.

"You and Crock-of-Shit are in deep freeze tonight, so bundle up. Get after it fast, and I'll switch you over to get some lumping done."

"Damn, Buck!" I say to him, but it's got nothing to do with the massive order he's just handed me. “You're dogging Harris, too?

“What? he asks innocently, “that's not his name?

“You're not right, I tell him. He sees me grinning and starts to laugh. I just shake my head and head back out of the office. Harris is still in the staff room, with his coffee still resting on his stomach. He perks up when he hears the door open up.

“What's the old man laughing about? he asks.

I look directly at Harris and say, “Nothing much.

His eyes move to the stack of orders on the clipboard.

“Aw hell, he says, “I know that doesn't say 'Deep Freeze' on it.

“Oh, so you do know how to read? I say. “Come on, man. Finish your coffee and let's get the hell on so we can get this done. I'm not trying to get frostbite tonight, so your ass better be moving.

He groans, throws back his cup, slams it on the table in front of him like he was taking a hard drink, and rolls off the chair in his effort to stand up. It's kind of pathetic to watch a man have to put so much work into just getting on his feet, but I try not to be too mad at him. I know he's got two little girls at home, and at least he comes to work so he can feed them half as good as he feeds himself. It isn't much, but at least it's something.

He does have his tricks though, and I wait for him to move first from the staff room. If you leave him behind, he'll find a way to get distracted and not make it into deep freeze for the first half hour or so. Some guys you have to keep in front of you, because you know what they'll do behind your back.

***

I function well in the cold. My body's lean, and I don't have as much insolation as a guy like Harris, but I still run pretty hot, anyway. Even in freezing temperatures, I can break a sweat if I work hard enough. Once the picking gets good on me, I'm finding all of the product I need fairly quickly and loading the pallets. Harris does his part and we create our system: I pick it and pile it, we wrap it, and he hauls it with the fork lift while I prep the next pallet.

His part of the system doesn't account for much action; I could do the lift part on my own, but Harris is still worth having around. The guy is a talker, and when you're working in deep freeze, they don't let you work alone in case of accidents, so the best thing you can do is to get paired up with someone who can carry a conversation. I've worked with some guys who don't do a damn thing and only know how to complain about how much the cold sucks, how much the job sucks, and how much their life sucks. I want to tell them to quit everything, then. Quit the job and go take a flying leap off a tall building. Harris might not do much, but at least he can talk some shit with you once in a while.

“Yeah, man,” he says to me, and his voice is full of disdain, “it's like she just keeps getting *bigger*, you know what I mean?”

“She just had your babies,” I tell him, slightly winded as I start to load up crates of ice cream. They're filled with the giant buckets of chocolate, strawberry, and vanilla combinations meant for birthday parties and family picnics; it's one of the worst orders you have to pick because they're heavy, so you have to bear hug them onto the pallet, which makes your arms start to feel numb pretty quickly. If you're not careful, you could drop a case and have a giant mess to clean up, which is more of a hassle than anything else. I look at Harris, just sitting in his lift, and I doubt he'd be any use in helping to clean up a mess tonight. It makes me wonder what his own place looks like. He's in his own world right now, staring off into nothing, like he's mulling over what I just said.

“I just miss the sex,” he says. “Like, we were banging back in high school, and out of nowhere she's pregnant and it's senior year, right?”

“Out of nowhere?” I ask him. “You *do* know how sex works, like biologically, right?”

He dismisses the question by not addressing it, continuing his little narrative. It's supposed to be a sob story, based on his tone, but I'm having trouble finding sympathy while wrapping the pallet of ice cream.

“A couple years out, baby number two comes along, and now here I am, twenty-two and working the graveyard shift, living in a trailer park. He looks like he needs to be slapped in the mouth, sounding pathetic the way he does. I smack the top of the pallet, trying to change the subject.

“Pallet’s wrapped and ready to roll, I say. “Let’s get it on.

“Let’s get it on, he echoes with a mock laugh. “You want to hear some shit, man?

I don’t, but he’s going to say it anyway.

“You know I’ve only ever been with one chick? he confides, and I’m not sure what reaction he’s looking for. Some guys would laugh, take the easiest insult that’s traveling through their head. Some guys might even show him some sympathy, I guess. Those things don’t make any sense to me, though.

I look at him hard for a second, and tell him, “Eh. You ain’t missing much.

This time his laugh is real. He gives a snort and says, “Yeah right, *Hound Dog*. With as many women as you’ve been with?

And this is when I start to hate the man. I don’t wear these women like they’re trophies. I don’t brag about any of it. If you stay quiet about a thing like that though, everyone wants to say something about it for you. Harris assumes I’m just being cool, but I’m not. I don’t do conquests. I just like to have sex, sometimes. It doesn’t mean I want a relationship, and most of the time, they probably don’t, either. I do them a favor by pulling the stunt I do the morning after. People act like I’m sabotaging a woman, but really I’m just sabotaging the obligation they feel to keep me around. Besides that, maybe one day I’ll have breakfast with a woman who finally surprises me and gives me a reason to try to surprise her.

“I’m telling you, man, I say, trying to dismiss his comment, “sleeping around ain’t all it’s cracked up to be. It’s not like one woman is wildly different from all the rest, you know what I mean? If you’ve had sex with one, you’ve basically had sex with them all."

"Yeah," he says, "but what about the *weird* stuff, like chicks that wear lingerie and all that?"

I shrug my shoulders. "The lights are usually off, dude, and by the end of it, people are just naked."

"Not my wife," he replies. "I tell her to keep her shirt *on.*"

"Wow," I tell him, "you might be the biggest asshole on the face of the planet."

He laughs, like what I just said was a private joke between the two of us, but it's not. I really do think he's terrible, and when he finally takes the lift and hauls the pallet to the loading dock, I'm happy to have a few moments away from him.

In a way, Harris Crockett is just another one of those people in my life that gives me some sense of validity. Is he really so cruel as to say things like that about the mother of his children just for a laugh, or is he being completely honest when he says this? She married him, didn't she, and bore two of his children? Is there something redeemable about him that I don't see at work, or is he just as bad at home? Does she feel just as trapped as he does?

I don't know the answers to these things, but I can feel myself internalize the scraps of his experience that I'm privy to, and it feels like I'm trying to justify something deep inside of me.

Five: Picked Up

When I think about my life, I catch an image of my Yaya when she used to take me to the pool when I was a little boy, years before Pop-Pop Mercier passed. This place we used to go to, the Conestoga Public Pool, was a nasty place. The shower stalls and changing rooms never looked like they were clean, and Yaya always used to yell at me for walking in there barefoot. It had two pools; one large and one small. The larger pool wasn't even all that big, either. It started at three feet at one end and went to five feet at the other end. There was no diving, and you could only do cannonballs and jack-knifes if one of the *cool* lifeguards were on duty. Worse though was when they'd blow the whistle and tell all the kids to get out for adult swim time. Sure, you could swim in the foot and a half deep kiddie pool if you wanted, but it always had really warm water, and you just knew it was for all the wrong reasons.

Yaya loved adult swim time. She'd hug her inflatable raft to her chest and politely dive onto the water head first, gliding to about the middle of the pool. There she'd float for the full thirty minutes of adult swim time, resting her head on her arms, and getting plenty of sun on her back. I remember getting anxious, just watching her out there all by herself, and I'd feel some kind of way about how she could just go off without me and have a good time. After not even ten minutes or so, I'd come up to the edge of the pool, with my toes curling over the lip of the cement, and I'd holler out to her, *"Yaya, what you doin'?"*

She wouldn't even open her eyes, but say, *"Yaya's drifting, baby. You go on in the kiddie pool if you want water. Yaya's gonna keep drifting until it's time to go.*

Another time at the same pool, I saw this kid in a grade under me jump into the deep end, and he didn't know how to swim, but it was like he didn't *know* he didn't know how to swim. He started flailing around, bobbing up and down in the water, and no one did anything at first, except the lifeguard on duty, who calmly hopped out of his tower, grabbed one of the long, thin metal poles that we were always told not to touch as kids, stuck it in the water, and swept it in a long soft arc along the top of the water until the side of it nudged the boy in the ribs. It wasn't anything like you'd see in the movies or on television, when the lifeguard does a nose dive off his tower and swims to the victim before putting him on his back to swim to safety. Instead, the kid grabbed onto the pole like he instinctively knew this was coming from a person ready to save his life, and the lifeguard just leaned into his back foot and hand-over-hand started pulling the boy toward the edge of the pool. When the kid got close enough to him, the lifeguard dropped to one knee, grabbed one wrist, put the pole down, grabbed the other wrist and then pinned them over top of each other on the side of the pool so the boy could stay up and catch his breath. The lifeguard spoke to him calmly, helped lift him out of the pool, and then got back in his tower, like nothing happened at all.

Those two memories of the pool do the best job of summing up where I'm at in life when I'm being completely honest with myself. Somedays, I feel like I'm that kid out in the middle of the water who thought he knew what he was doing but really didn't know how to swim at all, and I'm waiting for someone to come offer me a reach poll at the very least. Other days, I feel like I'm Yaya on top of an inflatable raft. I'm drifting and the sun's beaming down on me, and life is good. It used to be that that was all I ever felt, but lately there've been more drowning days that come sneaking up on me, and I never really know what to make of all that. I tell myself I'll figure it out sometime soon, but in the meantime, when I've got time, I go out to the bar and do some drifting.

I'm not a person that frequents the same bar every weekend. There are enough of them in the city that you don't have to do that, and besides, it's awkward running into a recent fling, and I try to avoid that in the first couple of weeks following the Breakfast Test. Baltimore is big, but it's not huge; sometimes you have to hit the road and drive to DC, and other times you need to drive up to one of the college towns outside of the city and hang out with *that* crowd.

York Road has a bunch of nice bars that are all in a neat little row on either side of one city block, and for the most part, it works. All of the drunks wind up in one concentrated area, and the older homes at the opposite end of the town don't have to worry about the noise. These bars tend to cater to younger crowds, or they try a classy pub approach to attract alumni and parents near campus intending to visit their children. Out of the dozen or so drinking establishments though, you'll find a tiny hole-in-the-wall that's mainly populated by angry locals who love to bitch about college students ruining their town. One of these bars is an old granite-walled joint called *Angel's Grotto,* and it's here that there's a little bit of a turf war going on. I didn't know that when I walked in, but I was quickly filled in on the whole thing.

The local rugby club has been looking for sponsors to help them pay for uniforms, and since Angel's has been trying to drum up business, they naturally offered to pay for jerseys and have offered to give discounted drinks to any rugger when they bring home a win. The townies feel like they've been betrayed, so they've been taking footage of guys in their rugby jerseys pounding shots and acting like idiots, and then sending it off to the university, hoping the club will get disbanded, which would be an end to the riff raff.

"I mean it, man, this guy Peter slurs into my ear; he's the one that's caught me up on the whole locals versus ruggers angle, and he says, "If I see just one old dude pointing a cell phone at me, *I am going to fuck him up.*

When I had walked into the bar, I only did so because I thought *Angel's Grotto* sounded like a solid name for a place, and I wasn't too interested in picking someone up for the night. If you go to one of the other joints a little further up the road, there are all kinds of college girls that are just waiting for someone to walk them back to their dorm room. It's not that kind of night for me, though. Sometimes, a guy just wants a drink in his hand and a television on in a public place where he can watch a fight and talk shit with the rest of the world. I came in, grabbed a seat at the bar, ordered a drink, and started watching a baseball game. I didn't realize that I was potentially in someone else's seat until I heard a voice say to me, "You're not Sean Don. Who the fuck are you?"

I looked around me, unsure of who the guy next to me was talking to, and I said to him, "Excuse me?" I could feel my heart start to pump a little harder, and the blood was getting a little mix of adrenaline. He was unfazed though.

"You a fuckin' local?" he asked me, and the way he was squinting, I couldn't tell if he was glaring or if he was just real drunk.

"Naw, man," I told him, "I'm from Bolton Hill. My name is Jimi."

"Good," he said, and then proceeded to fill me in on everything, right up to his threat to kick anyone's ass who tried to film him.

"Just let me see someone take video of me drinking this shot," he says, holding his glass up to eye level, "and I'll break the glass over their goddamn *face*. You know what I mean?"

He throws his drink back and slams the glass down onto the bar top. I give him a bemused smile. Everything after the moment he found out I was from Bolton Hill has been fun, and even a little educational.

"I'm over twenty one," he starts shouting to no one in particular, scanning the entirety of the bar, "and I'm wearing a rugby jersey! I'll drink if I want to! Go Tigers!"

"Go Tigers!" I shout back at him, and I raise my beer up to him. He looks back at me like he's just found a long lost brother, and he goes up for a high five, only to bring his whole arm down across my shoulders.

"I like you, man," he says to me. "You should come and play for our team."

"I can't, man," I tell him. "I don't go to your school."

"You should go to college and come play for our team," he tells me again, and I laugh.

"You got that kind of money on you? I ask him, and he earnestly starts patting his pockets, looking for his wallet.

"Why, you need some? he asks me, but before I can tell him I'm good, he pulls a vibrating cell phone out of his pocket and immediately straightens up when he answers it. I turn away and let him have his conversation, assuming that's the end of things. That's the thing about drunks; as fast as they decide you're a friend or an enemy, they're just as fast in deciding to forget you. But then, Pete lets me know otherwise.

"*No way, man,* he growls in the phone, "*We are* not *going to another bar. This is our* sponsor *bar. This is where the party's at. Get over here. Jimi and I are grabbing a booth.*"

I give him some side-eye, knowing the night has just taken a turn for the interesting.

"*Jimi!* he shouts into his phone, "*New recruit! Yeah, he's legit.*" He stares me up and down for a second, evaluating what he sees, before turning back away to continue his conversation. "*He looks like a wing. Get over here and we'll talk about it.*

He hangs up, and turns back toward me.

"That was Sean Don, he says, assuming I know who he's talking about. "Dipshit went to the wrong place. Come on, let's go grab a table.

This is how the night begins. My new friend Pete and I grab a table, sit across from each other, and we get to talking about life. It starts with lighter topics before turning toward the serious.

"I'm pre-law, Pete tells me, staring into his drink. At this point he's switched to beer, and had felt the need to explain to me tells me that he was doing so because he was a responsible drinker, and that all responsible drinkers follow the adage, *Liquor Before Beer, You're In The Clear.* He's contemplative now, and not as boisterous as when we first sat by each other at the bar top.

"Lawyers get paid pretty good, right? I say to him, but he just shrugs his shoulders.

“I guess so,” he says, “but a lot of people tell me it’s nearly impossible to find a job. It’s like everybody’s going into law school because they can’t find a job and they don’t know what they’re doing.”

“Is that why you’re in law school?” I ask, and he looks up from his drink with a slight knowing grin, as if we’ve been friends for years.

“Naw, man,” he says, “I just like to pick a fight. The courtroom is for when I want to argue and win, and rugby is for when I want to fuck somebody up.”

“You’re a bad man,” I tell him, and I mean it in the nicest way. If I were the type of person to stay put, I’d hang out with Pete more often. Why aren’t I that type of person, though? I try to think about who all I call a friend, like who I might call up to give me a hand if I needed to move, and I’m drawing a blank. I’ve got a ton of people who know me, or who know *about* me, but notoriety isn’t going to help you haul a couch up a flight of stairs.

“Bar keep!” I shout. “Can I get a shot of Jack over here, on the rocks?”

The outburst is sudden, and Pete smiles. “You sure as shit drink like a rugger,” he says, then asks, “So what do you do, if you’re not going to school here?”

I hesitate, but only slightly. I know that the beauty of keeping people at a distance is that you can always be honest with them and not worry about what they’ll think. It’s just that on the off-chance that I want to stick around; enroll in the school, take a couple of classes part time, join the team, make the friends, find the future... I never know if I should be embarrassed by what I do. I can never tell if it’s a mark against me. The feeling is fleeting, and I’ve already resolved myself to never come back to this bar.

“I do warehouse work,” I tell him confidently. “Third shift inside a freezer with a bunch of fuck-ups and ex-cons.”

“Damn,” Pete says, and he looks at me meaningfully, gripping his glass to take another drink. “That actually sounds kind of nice.

The look I give him must say a lot, because he follows up immediately with his explanation.

“I’m just saying the warehouse thing is nice, he says, “not the ex-cons thing. That probably sucks. But I know I’ve never had a problem with working with my hands.

“Hell, I say, “You want a job? I could get you on shift tomorrow night.

“Naw, he says, and he looks back into his beer glass again. He’s the type of drunk to go from one extreme to the other, and I doubt it will be too long before we come back to the personality of the guy who is happy to meet new people, or happy to beat their asses. For now, though, he looks like he’s flirting with darkness, as the intensity of the way that he stares at his drink continues to grow. “Dad used to do that kind of thing for a living. Told me *no son of his* was going to do the same. No offense, he adds, looking up at me, and I nod at him like there was none taken.

“Anyway, he continues, “my parents basically told me college wasn’t optional, even though I told them I don’t even know what I want to *do* with my life. Doesn’t matter. So I go to class, try hard not to fail, play rugby, drink, and I won’t think about anything else until I absolutely have to.

“I did a couple of years of community college, I tell him, opening up a little bit. “Just your basic English and math classes, though. I took a psychology class. I think I thought I was going to do something more, but the warehouse money was good and I pay the rent on time, so I figure I’m all right.

“That’s what I’m saying, Pete says, and he raises his drink to mine. “Life doesn’t have to be so complicated. I’d *kill* to not have all this college shit to worry about. Fuck studying, man. I just want to live my life.

We’re on the verge of a real understanding, I can see that. Just one step further and we take the awkward step of exchanging numbers so we can continue the conversation beyond today, maybe at another bar or in someone's dorm room while we watch a playoff game, but before that can happen, the doors to Angel's Grotto burst open, and a crowd of guys roll into the joint, and they're screaming, *"Heyo!"*

Pete jumps up from our booth and yells back, *"Heyo! Over here!"*

This is the point where I know I will fade into the background, surrounded by guys that already know each other and will carry on their own conversations without me, awkwardly eavesdropping on stories shared about people I will never meet, and I don't feel very much like being a fly on the wall tonight. I grab my drink and get up from the booth to take a seat back at the bar, but when I do, I feel a meaty hand grab me by the shoulder and spin me around.

"Yo, guys! This is Jimi!" Pete yells, throwing his arms back around my shoulders like we've been friends since way back when. "Does he look like a winger, or what?"

The band of them approach me, a few of them sizing me up, and one of them, a short and stout looking guy with a still-fresh rash just over his left eye, looks me over and asks me if I'm a runner.

"I've never run track or anything," I tell him, "but I guess I'm kind of fast. Like I used to play basketball, and I could get up and down court on a fast break pretty easy."

The guy stares at me for a second like he's making an evaluation, before thrusting his hand out toward me for a firm, if not overly strong hand shake. He reminds me of the type of little guy that has to show you how strong he is, just in case you mistake his height for weakness.

"Sean Donavan," he introduces himself, "Damn glad to meet you."

"Jimi Di Paola," I answer, "Right back at you. What happened to your face?" I ask him, nodding at his eye.

He touches the mark on his face, as if he wasn't exactly sure of what I was talking about. "Oh, this?" he asks? "It's nothing. I took a pretty good pop and my legs went up ass-over-kettle, and I got dragged by my face for a bit.

"Jesus, I say, and I can't help but give him a certain kind of look, "you guys don't wear any pads or anything?

"If you're worried about getting hit, Sean tells me, "just run faster than the guy trying to hit you. This must be an inside joke, because everyone starts laughing, and I can't help but smile in spite of myself. I didn't walk in here with any expectations, but the hour or so that I've been the bar has already been a pretty good time.

We sit down and order another round of drinks, and I get to hear from a lot of the guys. Some of them, like Pete, are serious students and they know they're going to be doctors and lawyers one day soon. Others are failing their classes, brag about showing up drunk, and how pissed their parents are that their tuition money is being flushed down the drain. Most of them worry about whether or not they'll find any type of job, and some of the guys get into a pretty heated argument about how much debt they're going to graduate with. All of them like to drink and sing what I guess are rugby songs, because they know all of the words by heart, and no one else in the bar seems to have heard a single one of them, myself included. I glance over at one older guy at the bar who looks like he's been giving the crew the stink eye-since they walked in, and it looks like he's fishing for his phone out of his pocket, and just as he's about to lift it up and point it toward the boys, the bartender walks over to him and places his hand on the old man's forearm and shakes his head at him. It looks like the turf war is real.

At one point in the singing, somebody messes up one of the songs, and he is immediately called out for it. Sean, who looks like he's some kind of captain of the squad, says to him, "Redeem thyself, and he looks around the rest of the bar to see if anybody's watching them. The man at the bar is distracted by the bartender; the one is arguing heatedly about loyalty to regular customers and the other is telling him about hard times. Everyone else is doing their best to stay oblivious, staring at their cell phones or the televisions mounted above their heads.

"Is he going to do it right here?" one of them asks, and it worries me that he's gone quiet in his tone. Pete sits up, and he seems a little more sober than he was, which is odd, considering how much I've seen him drink. Some people just know how to pull it together.

"Hell yes he's doing it right here," he says, and he's not exactly loud about it, but he's not quiet like the other guy is, either. "This is *our* bar now, gentlemen. He screws up the song, *he shoots the boot.*"

And now it starts to get strange. I never imagined myself sitting tonight in the corner of a large circular booth, crammed shoulder-to-shoulder with a bunch of guys I just met, but it's not that surprising, either. The night life can bring all kinds of interesting opportunities, and it's not unusual for temporary friendship to spring up like this. What *is* unusual, however, is when that large circle of guys you've been crammed into all start silently chanting the phrase "*Shoot the boot.*"

It starts off hushed and rhythmic, and the guy who just screwed up singing his verse of a song about how Jesus Christ can't play rugby takes off his shoe and reluctantly hands it to the person sitting next to him. The guy pours a splash of his beer into the shoe, and then spits in it, before handing it to Pete. Pete does the same thing; Sean gets it and drops nearly half of his rum and cola inside the shoe, followed by a real nasty wad of saliva. The shoe makes it all the way around, and when it gets to me, just two heads away from where the guy who started the whole thing is sitting, I just look at the others with a raised eyebrow and a bit of disgust on my face and pass it off. The guy to my left tries to hand it back to me, but Sean speaks up and tells him not to worry about it, that the shoe is nearly full anyway. So the shoe then gets handed back to the guy with a naked foot, and he stares into the sole of the thing, shaking his head like he knew better than to trust his own instincts about what the words to the song were.

Meanwhile, the table hasn't stopped chanting the phrase, and now it's getting louder and more rhythmic. Some of the guys are even slapping the table. The guy with the shoe closes his eyes, throws it back, and drinks the contents in one quick motion, before slamming it back down onto the table like it was a shot glass. He stands up in his seat and belts out his verse to the song, apparently flawless, and everyone else jumps back into the chorus with that much more revelry and even I can't help myself, having figured out the hook and being swept up into the spirit of the thing.

"Jesus saves, Jesus saves, Jesus sa-a-aves!

The song is over and Sean gets up and points to the guy that just drank out of his own shoe and raises his glass to him. He speaks boldly, and all of us, myself included, raise our drinks up with him.

"Here's to you and here's to me, and best friends we shall ever be, and if we should ever disagree, well then fuck you, here's to me!

It's a good toast, one I've never heard before, and I look at all the guys drinking together, and I feel something in this moment. They're relative strangers and have no problems being disgusting, evident by the guy who's putting his shoe back on, still soaked and stinking of booze, and best of all, I'm not too far off in life from the rest of them. Maybe everyone around my age is just drifting for the time being, and no one's really drowning, or if we are, we're doing our best to not let anyone notice. I can see the appeal of hanging out with guys like these on a regular basis.

Just then, the doors burst open again, and what comes through looks like every guy's fantasy – especially the way it complements the crowd I currently find myself in. A train of about nine women, some of them clearly buzzing, come through like they're part of some out-of-season Mardi Gras parade, and they are led by a round, but cute blonde with a kind smile, wearing a white veil and sash with silver letters covered in glitter that read "Bride-To-Be.

"Shit, boys, one of the guys says aloud, "it looks like we've got ourselves a bachelorette party.

Now, some days you don't go looking for opportunity, but it

tracks you down anyway, and taps you on the shoulder. I've experienced bachelorette parties before, and some of them can be just as depraved as bachelor parties. I've never been part of a wedding myself, and it could be because I keep things moving and don't typically cast the type of bond strong enough to warrant an invite to a wedding. Harris Crockett may have invited me to his wedding, had we known each other at the time, but it's probably for the best that we didn't, because knowing how I can feel about that guy sometimes, I more than likely would've RSVP'd only to not show up. That said, I can't say much about how wedding receptions go down, but I've run into enough of these types of parties to know two things: 1) They're easy to crash, and 2) It's easy to get laid.

I look around at all of the guys sitting near me, and it's interesting. Some of them look like they can't handle what's just happened, like they're not drunk enough to deal with the opportunity. Others are completely oblivious, still engaged in their own world, or maybe just too drunk themselves. A few look like they know what's up, though, and they're checking out everyone walking through. Classless.

The quickest route to sleeping alone is to look like a creep. Never mind the fact that I know I might really be a creep myself, at least I know how to *look* decent. When a situation like this presents itself, it's best to be cool. Be nice. Get out of the booth, and confidently approach the woman wearing the sash. I clear my throat lightly before I speak, extend my hand when she turns around, and I say to her:

"I don't mean to be rude, and please let me know if I'm intruding, but you look like a bride-to-be, and I just had to come over here and wish you congratulations, and offer you your first drink."

The smile on her face looks like it's a mile wide, and it hits me for the briefest of moments; she's genuinely in love. The way she lights up when I refer to her as the bride to be, and the way she takes my hand, like she's just so excited to confirm that she *is* the bachelorette, and that all of this is for her; all of it's like a quick gut-check, and seeing her expression plants a strange seed. Maybe monogamy isn't so bad.

"Thank you so much! she says to me, and you can tell she's feeling very bubbly. "I *am* getting married, and this *is* my bachelorette party.

"So then I *can* buy you a drink? I ask her, and one of her friends from the crowd of women, brown-skinned and beautiful, gets up on her toes so that her eyes come up over everyone else's, and she calls out to me.

"Why? You gonna put something in it? She's got the trace of an accent, like she's not naturally from around here, and the way she asks me this question, I can tell she's being playful.

"I wasn't planning on it, I reply, "but I could, if that's what you are into.

"She's not *nearly* drunk enough for you to know what she's into, the bride-to-be says to me, and I look at both of them, unable to contain a grin. This night just keeps getting better.

"I'd like to fix that, I tell the bachelorette, and I turn my attention to the bartender, who looks like he's just finishing up with the first of the women going up to order their drinks. "Excuse me, bartender? I say, "I'd like to buy two drinks, one for the lady, and one for her friend. Anything they want.

Just then, I feel a strong hand on my shoulder, and a fair bit of weight lean into me. I look to my right, just to see Pete, wide-eyed and starring at all of the ladies. Behind him are Sean and a few of the other rugby guys.

"We want to buy these girls drinks, too, Pete barks. All of the ladies in the party look over our way.

"Which ones? the bartender asks.

"All of them, Sean responds for him, and then turns his attention to the women. "Ladies! he shouts out to them, "We are the Fighting Tigers, and we will be your entertainment for the evening. Ask anyone of us to strip for you, and it's done, free of charge. The women in the party let out a loud cry, and now all of the guys are up out of their booth and moving toward them for a full on social.

The drinks begin pouring, and before it gets too crazy, I'm able to get the two beverages the ladies have requested. The bride-to-be gets a vodka cranberry, and when I hand it to her, she politely accepts it, but doesn't really engage in any type of conversation, which doesn't bother me in the slightest. One of the guys from the rugby team, Tommy, I think his name is, is talking her ear off about her wedding plans. I gather he's just proposed to someone himself, and the conversation he's having consists of what the cost of florists, photographers, and catering is like; it's all business, and the bachelorette seems happy to discuss everything. The two of them look completely engrossed with each other, and soon enough they'll be commiserating over being forced to overlook certain friends in favor of relatives they'd rather not see. It's not a conversation I'm interested in. I'm more interested in her friend, whose idea of a free drink is a cherry coke, with no alcohol whatsoever.

When I approach her, she's sitting at a table by herself, looking at everyone else having a good time, but she doesn't seem put off by any of this. She looks like she's happy that they're all happy.

"Cherry coke," I tell her, handing her the drink, "made to order."

"You spike this with anything?" she asks me, and I can't tell if she's being saucy or if she's serious. In spite of my usual confidence in these situations, I feel a nervous pang shoot up my stomach. I don't know that anyone's ever asked me if I spiked their drink before, and even if it's in jest, I think it bothers me that anyone might look at me in terms of being a predator.

"No ma'am," I tell her earnestly, just in case she too is being earnest. "I couldn't if I wanted to. I don't even carry aspirin on me."

"*Would you want to?*" she asks me with a raised eyebrow, and I feel that slight panic within me taken to a higher degree. The dynamics of this situation are slightly skewed, and I feel like I'm on my heels, but I don't know why.

"Would I want to? I ask with an immediacy that is the opposite of cool and collected. "Not unless I wanted to get the shit kicked out of me, I guess. A slight pause slips in after this, like that's my conclusion, and as soon as it registers that this is a terrible reason if it's the *only* reason I'm offering, I manage to sputter, "It's also a fucked up thing to do somebody, anyway. I mean mainly, obviously. Her look softens when I say this, and as an afterthought, I say to her somewhat sheepishly, "Sorry for my language.

Odd connections are being made inside my head. Any other woman on any other night, and I would've been on the good foot toward calling us a ride somewhere, but tonight is different. Am I talking to her because I just don't want to sleep alone tonight, or because I find her fascinating by way of an alluring first impression? She's not drinking, so there's nothing resembling the whole song and dance of two mutual strangers looking for lust under the veil of intoxication. She is with a party of friends, after all, and not so forlorn that she needs the company of a stranger. Likewise, if those are the details I'm picking up on, what does that say about me? I suddenly get a better sense of how much I've had to drink so far, and I'm dangerously close to getting sucked into the depressing headspace of existential questions whose answers are designed to make you feel worse and drink more. *Am I not that far removed from a guy who'd slip a pill in a woman's drink? What have I been doing with my life? Why doesn't my mother ask me about whether or not I'm going to find someone to settle down with anymore?* It's a quick and sickening feeling, and I think I'm ready to conclude the night's events and go home.

"My name's Jimi, I tell her, realizing I've just been standing there awkwardly while she sips on her drink, "Anyway, it was nice meeting you.

When I turn to leave, ready to sit in the car and contemplate how mortified this one moment has made me, she speaks up and catches my attention.

"You said your name is Jimi? she asks.

"Yeah, I tell her, turning back around to meet her eyes.

They look friendlier than they did a minute ago, and just like that, those existential questions start to dissipate. “Like the musician,” I say.

“Hendrix,” she nods, “Very cool.”

“You like Hendrix?” I ask her, and I take this as an opportunity to sit down next to her. More and more she doesn’t seem all that put off by my presence, and I can feel my mood improve just by being close to her.

“Sure,” she tells to me. “I listen to all that stuff - Hendrix, Clapton, Carlos Santana. All of those guys are great. It must be pretty nice to get to tell people you’re named after a musician like Jimi Hendrix. Do you spell it the same way?”

“I do, actually. That’s the way it’s spelled on my birth certificate. Not James, not John, just Jimi.”

She nods again in confirmation, and then looks back toward her friends, watching all of them get hit on by various rugby players, some repulsed and some countering with their own flirtation. In spite of successfully sharing a table with her, however, I’m still having trouble reading my own situation. We’re engaged in small talk, and she hasn’t been at all cold to my being right next to her, but at the same time she doesn’t seem interested in talking about herself, and I can’t tell if I should press on or just leave her alone. I sit with her for a half a minute, weighing my options, until I figure it might be best to go back to my original plan and just walk away.

“Well,” I say to her, getting up, “Enjoy your drink.”

“That’s it?” she asks, and I turn around once more. “You buy me a drink, tell me about your famous name, and you don’t even ask me for mine?”

“I didn’t want to kill your loner vibe,” I tell her, but I can see based on her expression that there’s something to work with after all.

“Not much of a loner tonight,” she says, motioning to all of her friends. “But someone’s got to be the responsible one, so here I am.”

"So that's why you're not drinking tonight? I ask her.

"That's why, she answers.

"Then I'm sorry for being rude! I say to her. It still feels like I'm fumbling for words, but at least the situation has improved. "I'll tell you what, I offer, "If you tell me your name, I can hang out with you and help you keep watch over your friends. I'll even flag myself and we'll be not-drunk together.

She smiles and says, "I'd like that. I sit back down next to her, and she extends her hand. "My name is Stefania, *Stefania Rosa,* but my friends call me Stef. I was named after my aunt.

"Does she play the guitar, too? I ask her, and this elicits a laugh from Stef. Then I follow up with that certain line, like it's out of habit, and I cringe when I hear the words come out of my mouth:

"So tell me something interesting about yourself.

She furrows her eyebrows, though, and shakes her head. "No way, man, she says. "Never trust a person who asks you for something interesting about themselves. It usually means they're fishing.

"*Fishing?* I ask, actually relieved by the way she's countered the question, even though it means she's got me figured out entirely.

"Fishing, she repeats. "Fishing for details, for things to talk about, or excuses to talk about themselves.

"You don't like to talk about yourself? I ask her.

"Do you? she replies.

And this is how we start off with each other. There are no pre-scripted conversations, because she destroys them all with this one swift moment. We're not drinking, and any buzz I collected from the alcohol with the rugby team is slowly starting to fade away. It happens naturally, without expectation, and the uncertain quality of where things will go feels better than when I'm usually talking to someone at the bar. It makes me wonder if I'm ready to give up all of the other canned lines and preplanned motions.

Six: Flipped

This is not like my other "next morning experiences, but it still feels incredibly awkward. We're not at Stefania's place, and we're not at my place, and we're certainly not in bed together. In fact, when I wake up, I'm on the couch by myself, and when I look over at the floor in front of me, I see one of the guys from the rugby team lying face down, fully clothed, with his head propped up on a small cushion that he's drooling on.

The only saving grace to waking up in such strange surroundings is that I remember *everything.* When we left Angel's Grotto, I was feeling fairly sober, though some of the other ladies in the party were less than themselves. Stef invited me and a couple of the other guys I'd met back to her friend Marie's place, because she lives in this big apartment-style dormitory, with four separate bedrooms and the living room that this guy and I fell asleep in. Since her other roommates were all away for the weekend, all had mutually agreed that everyone could save money on getting hotel rooms, and that their dorm space could host the bachelorette party, provided everyone would clean up after themselves.

When we had arrived, the party continued with card games and shots of fruity liquor. Because Stef wasn't drinking anything though, I also stayed away from the liquor. My mind was made up, and *she* was the one I wanted to keep pace with. A couple of the ladies were getting flirtatious with me last night, and it could've all been so easy, but Stef was the one I was drawn to, and all throughout the night, I kept getting to know her, bit by bit.

Maybe that's what makes this next morning all the more awkward. If I think about it, there's no need for excuses and nothing to apologize for. No one got laid last night, and no one's worrying about whether or not they've made a mistake. I don't know that I've ever been in this situation before, and I don't know what to do next. Should I just leave quietly? Sneak out like some shady dude who's guilty of something no one's sure of?

Should I stay and wait for Stefania to wake up? Would it be weird if I made myself at home? As I prop myself up on my elbows to think about it, Stef's voice, low and quiet, calls out to me, and I turn around to see where it's coming from.

She's standing in the kitchen, analyzing a can of coffee, and when she addresses me, it's with a level of comfort and familiarity that almost seems out of place.

"Hey," she says, keeping her tone hushed, "you drink coffee, right?"

"Yeah," I tell her, looking up at her while she still studies the can.

"So if I brew a half a pot, you'll have some, too?"

"Sure," I tell her, and she looks up at me with a mild flash in her eyes, like she just thought of something.

"You don't have somewhere else to be, like work or anything, do you?" she asks, and I wonder if this is the way she presses for more information about me, like who I am, and what I do.

"Nah," I tell her, "I'm working third-shift tonight, so I don't actually have to be at work until way late this evening."

She receives the information, but doesn't press for anymore. Instead, she turns around, opens up a cabinet behind her, and reaches up to the top shelf for two coffee cups. The counter top obscures her lower-half, but when she stretches out in just such a way, the bottom of her shirt rides up and I catch a glimpse of the small of her back, and it looks slender and delicate. Suddenly I feel really turned on, in spite of the fact that she's not wearing anything revealing or meaningfully sexy; just sweatpants and an old shirt, it looks like. Still, just the smallest bit of skin, and it feels like I'm ready to get there. I've got to get hold of myself.

I swing my legs off of the couch and over the guy sleeping on the floor so that I don't disturb him. When my feet are planted, I push off of the back cushion of the couch to kind of throw my body forward, and I have to pinwheel my arms when I almost lose my balance. Stef sees all of this and stifles a laugh.

"That's very considerate of you to not fall on top of the guy sleeping on the floor, she says. "You're very graceful.

"That's the first time I've ever heard that, I tell her as I approach the countertop. She has since poured a few scoops of grounds into a paper filter, added the water to the machine, and flipped the coffee maker on. By the time I sidle up to her, she's sitting at the counter on a small stool, and she pats the empty one next to her invitingly. I take the seat, and we both quietly stare at the coffee maker as it becomes the noisiest thing in the room, percolating and filling the immediate area with the smell of its fresh brew.

I have no idea how to proceed. We didn't have sex last night, didn't make out, and didn't even hug each other. I have no reason or room to just lean in and kiss her, but I want to, and more than that, I want her to want me to. She's got her chin in one hand, though, and the fingers of her other hand are lightly drumming along the counter top, like she's bored just waiting for the pot to fill. And so, I go to the same well I've gone to with all of the other women, and I tell myself that if she's cool about the bill, then I should just give in to the sappy quality of this whole "love at first sight thing that I'm experiencing, and make an honest go of pursuing a real relationship with her. In spite of the fact that I know I'm still operating with one foot out the door, it'll at least be the first time that I use the Breakfast Test for something beyond justifying my walking away from a one night stand, and for once I'll actually hope that someone passes so that I can justify a new thing happening in my life, and not a retread of what I've been doing with women for the past couple of years.

"Hey, do you want to run out and grab some breakfast with me? I ask her, smiling confidently, certain that this will go how I want it to. "I know this great little Cuban spot where we could grab a bite. My treat.

She turns her head sideways and gives me a funny look, but she's smiling too, so I know my offer's not completely out of the question.

"You trying to ask me out on a date or something? she asks.

"Is breakfast really a date?" I respond. She doesn't answer immediately, but studies me before letting her part of the conversation proceed.

"You just answered a question with a question," she says slowly, "Which really isn't an answer at all."

"So you want to know if I'm asking you out on a date?"

Having clarified that, she smiles again, and nods her head. Stefania Rosa is a brick wall and seemingly immune to all of my charm. I can't lay down a line to save my life around her, and with the way she keeping things aloof, it feels like I'm going to choke on my words if I continue down this path, so instead, I divert.

"Coffee's ready," I tell her, and I get up from the stool, walk around the counter top, and approach the two cups sitting near the pot. "How do you like it?"

Now her smile is showing teeth, and even in the morning, she looks good like this. I don't often think about a woman's teeth one way or another, but Stefania Rosa has really nice teeth.

"A little bit of milk and two sugars," she says. "How do you take yours?"

"*Café con leche,*" I tell her, and she laughs at me.

"I *know* you don't speak Spanish," she says.

"How can you tell all that?" I ask her, and she straightens herself like she's about to drop the facts.

"You don't have the accent for it *at all.* I grew up speaking Spanish, and you can tell the difference between someone who grew up with the language, and someone who went to a public school."

"Just like *that?*" I ask, opening up the kitchen refrigerator to pull out the carton of milk. "Then why don't you say something to me in Spanish and show me what you mean?"

"No," she says, and I stop what I'm doing.

"How come you won't speak Spanish to me?"

"Because I only speak the language to people who *understand* it. It's a matter of courtesy.

This woman has me figured out in a way that no other has ever bothered to try. I drop two sugar cubes in her cup, and rather than open random drawers, looking for a spoon, I swirl the cup around to try and get things to blend. When I offer the cup, she reaches out for it, and I pull it back slightly.

"If I give you the coffee, will you say something to me in Spanish?

She folds her hands together, taking on a look of sophistication, and gives me a perfunctory, "No. You don't speak the language.

"Fine, I reply, and inspired by the moment's flirtatious good will, I ask her, "If I give you the coffee, will you let me take you out on a date?

Her eyes narrow, and she studies me while I still keep her cup out of reach. I take a noisy sip of mine and tell her, "This coffee is damn good, too.

She smiles again, and says, "Deal, but I'm not interested in having you take me out to breakfast.

"Why not? I ask her, still withholding her cup of coffee.

"Because, she explains, "I can just make us breakfast after you help me clean up my friend's place.

The presumption of it all doesn't bother me in the slightest. "But you know I can't take you out tonight if I've got to go to work?

"Well then, I guess you'll have to make plans to see me again, right?

"Fair enough, I say, "It's a deal. Just know that I don't clean toilets, I tell her, handing her the cup of coffee.

She blows on it for a second and takes a sip, before looking up at me again.

"Don't worry, she says, "I'll teach you how.

***

As we drink our coffee, Stefania's friends come out to the

kitchen at various times, nursing varying degrees of one collective hangover. It's a rarity that I am not commiserating with them, but instead get to observe them as they go about their business. A few of the guys from the bar are amongst the people roaming the dormitory, including Pete, whom I say hello to, and who nods at me with the kind of look that says he has no idea who I am. It's not the first time I've made friends with people during the night and then had to re-introduce myself the next day, and I'm okay with this. As Pete's memories from last night fade away, so to will the comments about my enrolling in a university just so I could play a foreign sport with a bunch of guys I've only recently met. It's pretty crazy, the fantasies that men will create around a bottle of alcohol.

I'm following Stef's lead with how to handle the apartment. As people get dressed and leave, we drink a couple cups of coffee each, and we make small talk about the chores we had to do when we were kids. As the last people leave, she's assured people that they're free to go, since her new friend Jimi has volunteered to help her clean the place. By 9am, it's down to just the two of us in the dormitory, and while we finish the last of our cup of coffee, she tells me about how her parents were very strict about who did what when it came to household duties.

"Ladies clean the house and work in the kitchen," she says, and then switches to a gruff, masculine tone. "*Men work outside. Cut grass and chop wood.*" She sounds like she's doing an impersonation of a cave man, and it makes me chuckle.

"Wasn't like that at my place," I tell her. "It wasn't 'men did *this*; women did *that*.' It was just me and my mom, and we lived in an apartment. I don't even know how to use a lawn mower."

Her eyes grow wide. "Really?" she asks me.

"Yeah," I reply, mildly amused by her reaction. "Going outside was always to go play and get out of mom's hair. If I wasn't playing ball with people on my block, I was in my room, playing video games and stuff. I'd only know it was time to clean up when my mother would bust in, turn off the TV, and put on the music."

Her eyes narrow like I've just said something real. "You mean that's all it takes? she asks.

"All *what* takes? I respond.

"As in, all I have to do to get you to start moving is throw some music on?

I think about it for a second and tell her, "Only if it's the right kind of music.

"What kind of music did you and your mother listen to when you'd clean?

"We'd listen to Prince, I tell her, and she gives me a full smile. "You've probably got some Prince you're ready to put on, don't you? I ask her, and she nods her head before rushing off to another room. When she emerges, she's got her phone and a small speaker in hand, and in less than a minute, the room is filled with Prince's greatest hits.

A good groove can get anyone moving, and I'm convinced that that's all that Prince ever put out was music to *move* to – though I know he was probably talking about some *different* moves than cleaning a dorm. It still works for me though, and I'm into it. I start with the dishes while she does the laundry, and when she shows me where to find the bathroom cleaner, I also take care of the toilets, sinks, and tubs while she runs the vacuum, in spite of what I said earlier. The furniture gets straightened and even the windows get sprayed and wiped down. We knock it all out pretty quickly, and it's just a little past eleven when we put the cleaning supplies and the vacuum away.

"Not bad, she tells me, and she takes a deep breath in through her nose. "You can tell you've done a good job when the whole place just *smells* clean, you know what I mean?

"So we're all good then? I ask her, "We don't need to shampoo the carpets, too?

She playfully rolls her eyes upward like this is the sexiest thing she's ever heard. "If you tell me you do carpets, I'll lock you up and never let you leave.

“Ha ha,” I reply, flatly. “At this hour, I'll settle for taking you out to lunch. That's a fair compromise, right?”

“No, sir,” she tells me. “I promised you breakfast for helping me clean, and that's what's happening.”

“Well,” I tell her, “If you absolutely insist...”

And she does. I sit back to watch her work effortlessly, in someone else's kitchen no less. She takes eggs, ham, and cheese out of the refrigerator, and it feels like she's getting ready to do something really special. It's not impressive that she knows how to cook, but it's the *way* that she does it, like it all looks so graceful. She breaks eggs with quick decisive movements, and not a single loose shell falls into the bowl. Her wrist turns a whisk with quick beats, and she blends the salt, pepper, and cheese neatly, before pouring the mixture into the pan, where it cooks evenly. She knows when to fold in the ham that she's chopped into small cubes, and when she plates the final product, she makes sure to cut the omelet into two even halves; one for her, and one for me, and we both get two slices of butter wheat toast.

“Damn,” I say, fully impressed as she sets one plate in front of me before settling herself with her plate into the empty stool next to me at the kitchen counter.

“What is it?” she asks, and there's a note of concern in her voice. “You don't think it looks good?”

“No,” I tell her, “It's nothing like that.”

“Then what is it?” she asks again.

“It's nothing. I just can't remember the last time someone cooked something for me that looked this good.”

She doesn't say anything, but smiles at the compliment and quietly begins to eat her breakfast.

I've never known that a meal between two people could make feel such a way, and as if in response, a small bit of last night's unease comes creeping back to me while I'm chewing. I cannot believe I almost subjected Stefania to a thing like The Breakfast Test. I dwell on the subject a little longer while I chew my eggs, and I think about all of the girls like Caitlin that I went out of my way to piss off and scare away, just so I wouldn't have to share a quiet breakfast with them like the one I'm having with Stef. Had things gone differently, Stefania could have been just like the rest of them, through sheer force of habit and an invisible will to fuck things up for myself, and the whole thing makes for an odd moment of clarity. My saving grace might be that Stefania knew all of the right responses to every stupid line I could muster, and not a single one of them was the response I was hoping for.

Seven: Meet My Mother

Since that first day at her friend's dormitory, we've kept things to meeting up with each other at public places. We might meet at a bar with her friends, like when she invited me to the after party of her friend's wedding reception, or we might go to the park to hang out. She likes being outdoors and going for walks, so a lot of the time we just do laps around Patterson Park in the city and talk about movies, what's on television, and books that we've read. It never gets more personal than talking about how her classes are going, what's happening at the place she interns – things like that.

It's not all one sided, either. It's surprising to think that she even wants to know about what I do, to the point that she wants updates, and she even has her own opinions of Harris Crockett. She says things like *emotionally-stunted* when she describes his situation, and once she said she actually feels bad for him in a way.

"Men who treat their women like that, she says to me, "It usually has nothing to do with their woman. Something's wrong with them.

***

"Hound Dog! Harris says, *"My main man! You're alive!*

"What the *hell* are you talking about? I ask him, annoyed. "I know how to handle myself! He's late to work, and in my mind, he's talking about the company protocol. You don't go into deep freeze alone. If you get injured and they forget you're back there, you can freeze to death. You always hear the urban legend about somebody being found in deep freeze days after they've been reported missing, with frost on their face and a nose that's gone black, looking like it's ready to fall off. They peddle that story to the new guys, anyway, to get them to think twice about sneaking off by themselves to go and do something dumb. The job doesn't always attract the best and the brightest, hence my having to partner up with Harris. Buck put him on a different shift for a while, just to see if that improved his work ethic, but third shift has gotten thin lately, so I'm the lucky guy that gets to deal with a Crock-of-Shit and an infinite backlog of inventory.

Harris comes up from behind and pats me on the shoulder, like we're old friends. "Nah, man, he replies, "I know you've got it on lock back here. Always do. I just ain't seen you out at the bar in about a minute, and word is the *Hound Dog* found himself someone to put that leash on.

I roll my eyes. I felt like I knew this exchange was coming at some point, and it's just like I thought it would be. I just wish it weren't coming from Harris Crockett.

"First of all, I tell him, not breaking my stride and continuing on with my inventory, "I'm not trying to hear about anybody being on a leash. If you don't see me out at the bar or the club or anything, it's probably because you can't get into the places I get into, and anyway, I've been keeping busy.

"Yeah right, Harris says, "Busy doing *one* chick, or a bunch of them?

I stop what I'm doing and turn on my heel. "You *need* to check yourself and get the fuck up out of my face with that noise.

He takes a step back, puts his hands up in the air, and says, "My bad. I'm just playin' around. Just heard you were hooked up with a girl is all. No disrespect. He's smiling when he says this, but I can see a nervousness in his eyes, and that's good enough for me, so I turn back to my work.

"And so what if I'm hooked up? I add as an afterthought, "That's nobody's business but mine and hers.

"Shit, I think I know you better than that, Harris says, and he ambles beside me to start stacking boxes. This is how I know he feels like he's treading on dangerous territory with me. He's actually doing work.

I put down my clipboard and give him a hard look. "Now what's that supposed to mean? I ask him, and he gives me this innocent look, like he's just saying something casual.

“You’re a hound dog, man. You got the rep.”

“That’s an *overblown* rep,” I tell him, digging back into the inventory and feeling frustrated with myself.

“Maybe,” he continues, still cautiously, “but it’s hard to deny when you got a bunch of angry bitches collecting pictures and videos of you online...”

“Bitches?” I say, “Please. They’re consenting adults that want to get petty because they couldn’t show me the value in going on a second date.” Deep down, a part of me knows I could choke on my culpability, but there’s enough of an inherent fire in me to justify everything that I do.

“Fine,” Harris says, after a pause in the conversation. “Let me ask you this: Has this chick met your mom yet?”

“What’s that got to do with anything?” I ask him.

“Shit got real serious after I introduced my wife to my mother,” he says, “Then more so when I got introduced to her people. Life was over after that.”

“Well then rest assured,” I tell him, “my life ain’t over.”

You’d think I just told him Baltimore won the World Series. He starts jumping up and down, saying, “Ha! I knew it wasn’t serious! You’re still the same old *hound dog*!”

“Just shut up and let’s get back to work,” I tell him. “We’re backed up as it is.”

But the moment messes with me. It fills up my head and won’t let anything go. *Still the same old hound dog.* I don’t want to be anyone’s *dog,* let alone anyone’s *hound dog,* so whatever my reasons, whether just to spite Harris Crockett, or prove how serious I am about Stef, the result is just the same; it only takes six weeks for Stefania to meet my mother, and she’s game for it, too.

***

The first time I take Stefania to my place, it’s to show her the vinyl collection, and in the entire time I’m showing her each record and how my turntable works, the conversation never goes toward where I got the records from; she never asks about my father or my family at all, and she never brings up hers. It's just a place we never go. So, when I bring up taking her to meet my mother, I'm expecting some kind of surprise or shock or something, about how that might be taking things a little too fast. That's not what happens, though.

We're sitting on my couch, sharing a bowl of popcorn with a movie on, when I drop the idea on her.

"So, you're not gonna believe what *Harris* said to me at work last night... I say to her, and she reaches for the popcorn, but doesn't break away from the television.

"What's that fool got to say now? she asks me, and her voice is casual, like she's only got a passing interest in talking more about Harris Crockett.

"Man, he's trying to say we can't be serious about each other, because I haven't introduced you to my mother yet. I tell her, trying to keep myself just as casual as she is.

She's still looking at the television, completely unfazed. "Let's go meet your mother, then, she replies in this dull sort of voice, like without any emotion at all, and just like that, it's settled.

Now as casual as that sounds, it's *just as casual* when I tell my mom that I'm bringing a girl over for our Sunday visit.

"Huh, she says when she hears me tell her over the phone, "Guess I better cook something decent then. Maybe run the vacuum before you stop by.

I don't know why I think it's supposed to be a bigger deal than what it ends up being with Stef and my mother. To them, I guess it's just the next logical step. For me, though, it feels like a gigantic leap.

***

Sunday morning comes around, and I pull up to Stef's place for the first time. She lives just off her campus in the Donning-Brookes Complex, which is like a series of small houses that are designed to be apartments. I'm familiar with the area, because I've been around for a rendezvous once or twice before; familiar enough to know that if you've walked through one of the buildings, you've walked through *all* of the buildings. They're a lot of two-story affairs that've been sub-divided to make up four apartments; two on the basement level and two on the ground level. Beyond the common front lawn and walkway, each apartment gets to maintain some degree of autonomy; no shared hallways or bathrooms, and each has its own "front door" to lock as a tenant sees fit. The apartments themselves aren't too shabby on the inside, either. Stef looks like she lives in one of the bigger places; probably a two bedroom, one bathroom flat, with a small kitchen and a living room that doubles as a dining room if you set it up the right way, and I start to imagine how she might have her place situated.

That thought, though, brings up a bigger, scarier thought; what if she asks me inside? What if I get recognized by some girl I once hooked up with? Would I be called out in public? Would someone start whispering in Stef's ear when I wasn't around? The thought makes me squirm a little bit, and I lay on the horn for a second to let her know I'm out front, so I don't have to get out of the car.

A moment passes, and I see the front door open before Stef comes out, looking gorgeous. Her hair is tied back in a way that shows off her long, slender neck, decorated by a strand of pearls, and she's got this light blue dress on that really brings out the deep brown of her skin. The skirt comes down to just past her knees, but even still, the white heels she's wearing makes what you can see of her legs look taut and lean. The only thing throwing her whole aura off is the look she's shooting me as she approaches the car.

"What's the matter?" she asks when she opens the door and climbs into the front seat. "You can't get out of the car and knock on the door to escort a lady to a vehicle?"

"Damn!" I say, and I can't help but smile at her. Even when she's pissed off, she still looks pretty to me. "I didn't know it was a crime to stay in the car and honk for you."

She glares at me for a second. "It's *not* a crime when it's a regular car with a regular sounding horn, she tells me. “It’s *annoying* when the car’s a giant Buick that sounds like it has a *fog-horn* going off.

“It may as well sound like that, I say, putting the car in drive. “If you’re going to drive something that’s as big as a boat, it makes sense that it would sound like one, too.

She doesn’t appreciate the humor, though; nor does she appreciate my driving. To get to my mother’s place, you’ve got to go through the back roads, and sometimes they force you to weave side to side while you go through a bunch of rolling dips. I’ve driven the roads before, and I know how my ride handles; my tendency is to take these turns at the highest speed you can get to before losing control, hugging the side of the road instead of winding up in the trees or in a ditch somewhere. That’s how *I* always drive, anyway. It doesn’t take me long, however, to notice that every time I take one of these turns, I can see Stef’s hand reach for the grip on the door, squeezing tight for each dip. Soon, her other hand is clenched around the side of the seat, and I can feel it setting off something inside of me that I can’t properly explain. When I see her tense up completely, though, I can feel my foot pressing just a little bit harder on the gas.

“Jimi! she finally breaks, “Could you please take it easy on these turns?

“What’s the matter? I say to her, keeping my voice casual, “You don’t like my driving?

“That depends, she groans, still holding tight to the seat and the hand-grip, “Do you like me getting sick and vomiting all over the front seat of your car?

“Oh, shit, I tell her, “I didn’t realize it’s that kind of situation. The sudden guilt I feel rocks my stomach, and I pump the breaks. She opens the car door while it’s still in motion, and I pull over on the side of the road, just in time for her to unbuckle and lean out of the car. When she starts to wretch, there’s no way to account for how terrible I feel, and when she asks me, still leaning her head out the car door, to dig into her purse for a couple of tissues, I practically tear the thing in half, I’m scrambling so hard to get her what she wants.

She takes the tissues, wipes her mouth, and throws the trash into the grass on the side of the road. She sits up, pulls the passenger-side visor down and opens its vanity mirror to check her make-up and adjust her hair. I watch her get collected, unaware that I'm just as tense as she was when I was driving the car, and when she calmly buckles her seatbelt, I start stammering all over myself.

"Shit," I tell her, "I am so- I didn't know you get car-sick..."

"Jimi," she breathes calmly, "We're okay. It's not like you did it on purpose."

She's not messing with me when she says this, but is being completely honest, and it hits me harder than if she was trying to be a bitch to me. Here I am, driving like an asshole, and for what? To make some kind of point? I saw her getting tense, so why did I have to start driving like an even *bigger* asshole? What the hell is wrong with me?

"Besides," she continues, "I don't think I've ever gotten sick in a car before, so if anyone feels bad, it's me. Sorry it was in your car and not mine."

"Nah," I tell her, "We're okay. You got it outside the car, and not inside, so there's nothing to apologize for. Do you still want to go to my mom's, or are you trying to go back home?"

"No, no," she says, popping a mint from her purse into her mouth before grabbing a tube of lipstick to reapply while still studying herself in the mirror. "We're in the car, we're on the way, and I've just done one of the most embarrassing things I can think to do in front of you. If anything, meeting your mother should be a breeze for me now."

I put the car back into drive and we continue on in silence, both of us feeling awkward for our roles in her roadside sickness, though she's got no idea that I was driving like that on purpose. What did I think was going to happen? It bothers me, like I know I've caught a glimpse of something ugly about myself and I'm not sure what to do about it, and meanwhile,

Stef's in the passenger seat feeling guilty for something I'm to blame for. I could apologize to her. I could tell her I feel like it's my fault; come clean and be honest. I don't, though. We just sit in silence, and the next words that are uttered are the ones from my mother when she opens the door to greet us in front of her home.

"*Hello!* my mother says, opening the door, and there's a bounce to her voice that betrays how casual she was over the phone about meeting Stef. It must be infectious, too, because, the smile that Stef gives her could melt a glacier, and they give each other this hug like they're old friends. Meanwhile, I'm just standing behind them with my hands in my pockets, watching the whole thing go down, and a rock feels like it's starting to form in my stomach.

"It's lovely to meet you, Miss Di Paola, Stef says, and my mother quickly corrects her.

"Please, she says, "Call me Vivian.

"Okay! Stef answers her in a brilliant tone, and I think it's because she's happy to not meet a woman who is confrontational about her son. Italian mothers get this weird sort of stigma about the way they handle their sons, and although we never talked about it, I'm willing to bet that Stef had some reservations. Hell, maybe *that's* what made her get sick in the car – just the nerves of meeting someone like my mother, but the thought isn't enough to alleviate the guilt I feel for driving like an asshole on purpose. "You can call me Stef, she continues, and mom places her hand on the small of her back, gently guiding her to the front door.

"Hi, Mom, I say to her when she throws a glance toward me, and I see the smile melt from her face, turning into the look that I remember from when I was a teenager.

"So, Jimi, my mother replies as we make our way into the house, "How long have you been hiding Stef from me?

"Six weeks, Stef answers for me, and my mother pauses in her stride and glares at me for a second.

"Six weeks? she asks, astonished. "What the hell took you so long?'

I can't say anything in response, and I don't need to. Stef's appreciative laugh fills the room, and it's response enough, like she's charmed by the thought of mom getting pissed at me for not bringing her home sooner.

"You know, he's never brought a woman home to meet me before," my mother whispers to Stef, except it's not really a whisper at all, because I can totally hear her. *"You'd think he was ashamed of me or something.'*

"Not at all, Mom,' I tell her. "I was just waiting for the renovations to get finished.'

"He's *so* thoughtful, my mom says, but Stef overlooks the sarcasm as she walks into the kitchen, admiring everything around her.

"Have you recently remodeled?' she asks, and my mother takes a seat at the table, taking the opportunity to look at all of the things Stef observed, like she wants to reconfirm all of her own evaluations of everything she's done to the place.

"Yeah,' she says, "a little here and a little there. Me and some of my girlfriends did the flooring, put a fresh coat of paint on the walls. We put in a couple of ceiling fans,' and she looks up to the fan directly over her head when she says this. I look at it too, and from where I'm standing, it looks like it's spinning with a slight wobble, so that if the room were completely silent, there'd be a creaking sound that would probably annoy me if I had to live here by myself. When Stef looks at it, though, she looks like she's appreciating a work of art, and she grabs a seat next to my mother, and puts her hand over mom's wrist.

"*You* did all of this?' she asks, and she sounds really enthused by the idea that my mom is a living example of female-empowerment. I'm still standing off to the side, watching the exchange, and it makes feel a little like being an outsider.

My mother looks directly at Stef and tells her in a very serious tone, "You'd be surprised what you can do when you've got a bottle of wine and a couple of girlfriends who like to drink.

"So you like wine? Stef asks, and then she sounds upset with herself. "If I'd have known, I would've had Jimi stop somewhere so we could bring a bottle for dinner.

"Oh no, Mom tells her, "The wine is for my girls. I haven't had a drink in... and she trails off for a second like she's trying to run the numbers before looking at me to ask, "How long has it been, Jimi?

Jesus Christ, Mom, I think to myself, *Way to throw her in the deep end and we haven't even been in the door for five minutes.*

"It's been a long time, I say, and I hope she gets it, that I don't want to go there in the slightest.

"A *very* long time, she echoes, looking back at Stef, "but, don't let that bother you. I've actually got a bottle here that one of my girlfriends left behind the last time I had people over, and I think it would go perfectly with dinner.

"What are you making, Mom? I ask, joining them at the table, happy to shift the topic away from anything that could turn remotely revelatory.

"Chicken Piccata, she says, "Just like when you were little.

I cannot remember the last time I had Chicken Piccata with my mother. If I think hard enough, though, a memory surfaces of a rare instance when Yaya visited us in the apartment, and the three of us sat together and ate my favorite kind of chicken dinner. I was happy, and they were civil.

"I've never had it, Stef says, and Mom smiles at her.

"Well, there's a first for everything, she tells her, "and if you don't mind giving me a hand, I'll even show you how to make it.

***

The food prep gets along easy enough with three people in the kitchen. Mom hands me a package of red potatoes and says no more. I slice them thin, lay them on a baking sheet, and coat them with an olive-oil, salt, and pepper mix, while Mom and Stef ready the chicken and discuss what capers are, and where the hell you can even find them in grocery stores, anymore.

"I swear to you," my mother says, "It's like they don't even want you to buy *real* food at a grocery store. You have to go to all these specialty stores or farmer's markets..."

While they keep the conversation going, back and forth, it occurs to me that I'm being abnormally quiet, and I realize that I can't remember ever seeing my mother look so pleasantly social. I've never been invited to her renovation parties, so maybe I just don't know my mother all that well anymore. Maybe she's been like this for a while. When it's just the two of us, though, it's never this energetic. I should be happy that they're getting along okay, sure, but for every friendly exchange they keep having, I can feel myself pulling inward, staying quiet, never cutting in on their conversation, and absorbing the sounds of their voices.

It doesn't get any better when we sit down to eat, either. The two of them jump all over the place, and I keep my mouth shut, learning more about them than I ever thought I would over one simple Sunday dinner. In between bites of chicken, potatoes, and green beans, they discuss their college experience.

"Oh, you know I think it was still a little different back then, though. I was just happy to get the two year degree and keep a steady job in the hospital. We still didn't have a lot of women in the classroom, yet."

"Really? It feels like all I've ever seen are women in my classrooms. I don't even know what classes all the guys in my major are taking..."

"*If they're even going to class...*" (And she slides me a knowing look, while all I can do is just shake my head. Good one, Mom.)

They discuss their favorite exercise classes.

"You're taking a pilates class?"

"Well, it's a pilates class on Tuesdays, and then a beginner's yoga class on Thursdays. One of my girlfriends convinced me to go, and it really has been doing some wonders for me, you know? Like, I'm just more conscientious of what I put into my body, because the older I get, the harder it all gets to just *feel good,* let alone *look good.*"

"But at least you're *doing* it. They offer classes on campus, but I always talk myself out of going for one reason or another. Like there's always the equipment you have to bring..."

"...Oh, the equipment is nothing. You just need a yoga mat and that's it. I've got an extra one in the closet that you can just *have.* You can take it with you when you and Jimi are on your way out."

They have clean plates in front of them, and my food is barely touched.

"What's wrong, Jimi?" my mother asks me. "You feeling okay?"

"Eh," I tell her, "Just don't have much of an appetite right now."

"Was he a picky eater when he was little?" Stef asks my mother, and you can tell she's eager to catch some details of me as a child.

"Nope," my mother replies, thoughtfully. "Though, he really couldn't afford to be, truth be told. It was always just the two of us, so he didn't really have too many choices."

I feel the conversation getting heavier.

"It wasn't *always* just the two of us," I reply, and I can hear a sourness in my voice that I didn't mean to have. My mother hears it, but stays remarkably even-tempered; it used to be that a subject could set her off, but the older she's gotten, the more she's able to maintain a steady calm, like she's been around for a while, and nothing's new for her.

"No, you're right," she says, nodding slowly. "We did always have visits with Yaya."

It hits me in a way when she uses the word *we.* It's not something I'd ever expect from her. Stef is completely unaware of the moment, though, and presses on.

"Who is Yaya?" she asks, and my mother's hand flashes quickly, striking me against the arm.

"Don't you share *anything* with this young lady, Jimi?" and once again, I hear Stef laugh, like she's pleased to see such strength in a woman.

"I just never thought to bring it up! I tell her defensively, rubbing the spot where she hit me.

"Yaya, *Yvette,* was Jimi's grandmother, Mom explains, ignoring my tone. "She died when Jimi was in high school. He had his grandfather when he was a little boy, but Yvette's husband passed away early on, so he really only had a strong relationship with her growing up. He never got to meet my parents, either. They died in a car accident when I was in college. She pauses for a second, then adds, thoughtfully, "I was probably around your age when it happened.

It's a strange thing that occurs, but it's the first time that I see Stefania with tears in her eyes. My mother is equally alarmed.

"Oh my goodness, she says, "Was it something I said?

"No, no, Stef answers, and I can her voice breaking, "It's just... you remind me of how I lost my parents.

"Oh, honey, my mother says, and takes Stef's hand in both of hers, "I had *no* idea! Jimi certainly never brought it up to me.

I feel a jolt in my stomach, and I know that I'm guilty for being completely unaware of her family situation. Six weeks, and I never even thought to ask her what the story of her life was.

"He wouldn't know, Stef says, stifling tears while wiping away what's falling with her free hand. "I don't go out of my way to talk to people about it. You just caught me off guard is all.

For the next hour, I sit in my continued silence while Stef and my mother engage in this in-depth conversation about what it's like to grow up as young women without parents. The conversation is humorless, but intimate. Their struggles are remarkably similar, and they connect with each other on such a level that it's like intruding on the conversation of two old friends. It's weird, feeling like an outsider at my own mother's table, but that's exactly how I've felt this whole time. I should be relieved that they're getting along the way that they are, but I feel a sense of dread that my face can't conceal. When Stef looks at me, after pouring her heart out to my mother, she shifts around in her seat and then excuses herself to use the bathroom. Mom and I watch her get up and move away from the kitchen, and when we hear the door to the bathroom click shut, my mother gives me the full stare down.

"Jimi Andrew Di Paola, she says, using the full name like I'm still just a child that needs to be told about myself, "Have you shared a *bed* with this young woman?

"Christ, Ma! I tell her, "What kind of a question is *that*?

"I'm telling you right now, son, my mother replies, "You *cannot* share your body with a person and not share the rest of yourself. You've been seeing her for almost two months and you don't know anything about her *people*?

"I didn't think to ask! is the only thing I can say to her.

"That's because you don't *think*, she says, getting up to go put the kettle on, and once again, I'm left quiet.

When Stef comes back from the bathroom, she sits down next to me, and my mother busies herself with fixing cups of tea. Stef and I stay silent, but she does a thing that I'm not expecting. Without ever making eye contact with me, she reaches over and grabs my hand, and just holds it, right there on top of the kitchen table for anyone to see. When my mom brings the tea over, she notices it, and I can see something flash across her face.

This is how our visit ends. The conversation stays light while we sip our tea and Stef and mom nibble on some of the cookies sitting in front of us. I only drink; my stomach just won't feel right.

***

It's dark when we leave. My mother gives us both a big squeeze, and she tells Stefania to come back and see her anytime. When we drive through the hills back to her place, I make sure to set the cruise control, and I do my best to take it easy on the turns. The radio stays off, and we drive in silence.

"I'm sorry I never asked about your parents or anything, I

tell her when we're half way back to her apartment. "I feel really shitty about that.

"Please don't, she says, and she means it in the nicest way. "It takes two to talk. You don't ask. I don't tell. Honestly, until tonight, I didn't know how serious we were going to be, you know?

I don't take it as an insult. I know exactly what she means.

"Well, you met my mother, so I guess it's a thing now, right?

The line gets a small laugh, but I can't tell if the tension in breaking or building. There's something out in the open – I know it. For the first time, I feel like I want to talk about something, and not just use it as a means to an end, but really say something to somebody that means more than most.

"My father's in jail, I say, and the nakedness of the fact feels like it's echoing in the silence of the car. "He was around when I was a baby and everything, but I don't really remember him at all. He's serving a thirty year sentence.

Stef doesn't say anything, and the silence keeps on.

"Just thought you should know, I continue, and it all feels clumsy to me as I hear the words coming out of my mouth. "You know, cause of everything...

"Do you ever visit him? It's a simple question that she asks, but strikes at me in a way I don't see coming. I've never had a woman ask me before. I've *told* lots of girls about my dad, but it was always to help me with a pick up, like my damaged goods are attractive to strangers, somehow, but this feels different. It feels like I'm talking about a weakness that I've never been able to confront.

"Nah, I tell her, "What he did was pretty grimy. He broke into my mom's work to steal a doctor's prescription pad, and he got busted getting fake prescriptions filled when one of his pill head friends OD'd on his stash. Mom almost lost her job over it, but my father confessed that she didn't know anything about it, and a security guard who was in on the thing backed the claim up. It was touch and go for a little while, though.

Silence fills the car for a minute, like I need to soak in that reality, too. "I don't know what my mom really saw in him," I add. "I think she thought she could fix him or something."

"Well, thank God you have your mother, then," Stef tells me, and once again, her hand falls over mine. We're quiet again for another minute, and then she turns to me and says, "I'm sorry I've never had you over my apartment."

It's a comment I wasn't expecting. "That's no big deal," I tell her. "Feels like it took me forever to get you into mine." It's true, too. The first couple of times we hooked up were once in the back of my car and at the hotel room from when her friend got married. It took a month for her to stay the night at my place.

"Yeah, well," she says, "You don't have any roommates. I do."

"What, you got an uptight chick you have to share a bedroom with or something?" I ask.

"More like my little brother," she says.

"Oh," I tell her, and it dawns on me now how sensitive all of it is; no parents, but Stefania and her younger brother having to live together in an off-campus apartment. It could be tense bringing a guy over. "Well, I mean, since you've met my people..." I start, and she cuts me off in mid-sentence.

"Next week," she says. "Drop me off at my apartment tonight, and next week you can come in, have dinner with me, and meet my little brother."

"That sounds nice," I tell her, and I finish the drive in silence, turning the thought over in my head as we get closer to her place. Unexpectedly, it really does sound nice to me.

Eight: A Long Time Coming

At what point do you figure that you've become an adult? When you're a kid, people make it sound like there's some kind of magic line that you cross, and you only eventually find out that there isn't. The first few hallmarks make it all seem pretty simple, though, like, "Congratulations on your first chest hair; now here's your first kiss, and don't be late for losing your virginity, because that's coming quicker than you think..."

At thirteen, I was allowed to go into certain kinds of movies without my mom.

At sixteen, I was allowed to drive a car.

At seventeen, I was allowed to go into *all* kinds of movies, definitely without my mom.

At eighteen, I was allowed to vote, die for my country, and get drunk in Canada.

At twenty-one, I was allowed to get drunk at home.

All of these numbers, though, they're just birthday parties that are tired and played out. They're not an accomplishment of any kind. They each go from feeling like the holy grail of growing up to becoming arbitrary, and almost instantaneously. I remember being excited to finally become a teenager, just so I could hang out with the cool kids and feel like I belong and not be treated like a baby because I was only twelve, and I was *just* as excited when I turned twenty, only so I could tell everyone I was done with being a teenager, and all of the terrible people I thought were the cool kids. In hindsight, the joy of turning twenty is hilarious; being twenty may as well just be a second year of being nineteen, for all of the things it allows you to do, and a year later, once you reach the last milestone, you can't help but feel lost. There's no recommended age for when to get married, have kids, or die. It's all uncharted, and it stays that way for each person that gets to come up in the world.

Add up all these milestones, and you'll realize you just have a list of symptoms that indicate the onset of adulthood. That's what it is for me, anyway. Finding out you've become an adult is exactly like finding out you're sick. By the time you recognize it, it's already done and too late. I remember the first time I checked out a woman's left hand to see if she was wearing a ring before I tried to talk her up. I looked without thinking about it, but it hit me hard when I recognized her naked finger, and why that was an important new step in the process of hooking up with somebody. It wasn't a conscientious decision, but it was an important one to make, like I recognized that I was swimming in new waters, where some of these women had already been caught and tagged. A pissed off boyfriend isn't fun to deal with, but I've always made sure never to go at it with a pissed off husband. Some lines aren't worth crossing, and that's one of them.

Of course, there are other symptoms, too. People everywhere probably have a moment that really makes them pause and say *Damn, I must be getting older* at least once in their lives; like when they turn on a cartoon for the first time in forever and it doesn't give them the same sense of joy, or when they stop drinking chocolate milk and switch over to some frou-frou coffee beverage. Sure, they might try to pick up a bottle of chocolate milk later in life, but it's guaranteed that they'll only drink half of it before being overwhelmed by the flavor. Maybe by then, they'll have a kid in their life that they give the rest of it to, and then the whole cycle just repeats itself.

I'm experiencing a symptom of adulthood now, and it's fucking with me. Stef invites me over to her place for an early afternoon dinner with her family, and I'll be the oldest person in the room. By default, that makes me the adult. What's more, it's not going to be like a college house party vibe or anything, where we order pizza and split a dirty thirty case of the cheap stuff. She's got a whole menu planned out, and this is supposed to be one of those classy affairs that has lit candles and background music. I know, because she wants me to bring over my copies of Santana's first two albums, *Santana* and *Abraxas.*

"Are you really trying to have music playing while we eat?" I ask her, and she nods her head emphatically.

"*Black Magic Woman* and *Oye Como Va* are perfect for polite company. It's not like we're going to blast it, and anyway, Arturo only got his turntable like a week ago and I already told him you collect vinyl. He's excited to talk about what you have.

Arturo is her brother. From everything I've gathered about him so far, he seems like a pretty decent dude. Twenty years old and he's working two jobs, plus doing under the table work on the weekends. He and his sister have an arrangement all figured out. He can help take care of living expenses while she finishes up her nursing degree, and when she gets a job, it'll be his turn to take classes. I know he wants to go to culinary school, and eventually land a job at an upscale restaurant. I've studied up on Arturo. I want him to like me.

When I show up to her place, I'm wearing khaki slacks and a buttoned shirt, hugging *Santana* and *Abraxas* to my chest. Stef opens the door, and she's got on a yellow and black polka dot dress, and her hair is pinned up behind her ears. She's so beautiful, I feel under-dressed.

"Man, I tell her, "You've got me looking like a bum.

"Absolutely not, she says, and she leans in to kiss my lips before escorting me into her apartment. "You clean up pretty nicely.

"Yeah, I say, "but maybe your brother's got a tie or something I could borrow?

She laughs. "What, are you feeling insecure or something?

"I might be a little nervous, yeah, I admit to her, "But it's not like I was throwing up outside my car or anything.

"Oh please, she retorts, as I follow her into the kitchen, "That had nothing to do with meeting your mother. I've just been battling a stomach thing for the past couple of days.

"You aren't sick right now, are you? I ask.

"Not really, she says. "A little this morning, but I feel pretty good now.

"Saltines and ginger ale is all I ever eat when I'm feeling sick, I tell her. "You want me to run out and get you some?

"That's so sweet, Jimi! she says, "But that's not what's on the menu. My brother's room is just over there to the left. She points to a closed door behind me, just beyond what looks like a common area that's been set up to be a nice dining room. "His record player is in there. You can put the record on now if you'd like, and while you're in there, you can borrow one of his ties if you want. He's got a ton of black and grey ones from waiting tables.

When I walk into Arturo's room, I start to case the place; not like what I tell women I do with bars and stuff, as if I'm looking for what cool things I'd try to steal if I thought I could get away with it, but more the way a cop might look a place over. Everything feels like it's a clue.

For instance, his bed doesn't look like it's been made for a month, but he doesn't have any laundry on the floor, either, so you might say he puts in at least some effort in terms of him keeping his part of the house together. That makes him respectful, probably, and maybe even a half-way decent brother. Likewise, he's got an old computer that looks like it came from the stone-age on his desk, but it's got a new gaming controller hooked up to it, which means he might be one of those hardcore gamers that you sometimes hear about. The books lined up neatly beside the monitor suggest as much; they interchange between copies of different gaming manuals and strategy guides, interspersed with a couple of worn-out cook books with notes sticking out of the pages at random intervals.

"This dude takes cooking seriously, I say to myself, and I continue to scan the room, taking in the walls for any additional information. There are no pictures, with the exception of a giant-sized poster of Manu Chao. I don't know what it is, but it's colorful, and looks like it might be for a Spanish rock band. It makes sense, because it's right above the little table next to Arturo's bed, and this is where he keeps his record player.

Underneath the table is a small plastic crate that looks like it's seen better days, and inside of it are a few a records that look even worse than the crate. A Led Zepplin album looks like it's slowly disintegrating, and there's an Aerosmith album that only looks slightly better. Beyond those are copies of some blues albums I've never heard of, and a few scratched up CD cases, some belonging to singers I'm familiar with, like Enrique Iglesias and Shakira, others I've never heard of, like Prince Royce and Romeo Santos. One CD catches my eye belonging to a band called Farofa Carioca, and I stare at it for a second before putting it back with the rest of his minimal collection.

"Thank God for Zepplin and Aerosmith, I say quietly as I unsleeve the *Abraxas* album and place it lightly on the turntable. "At least we'll have *something* to talk about.

I turn the player on and gently set the needle into the groove before setting down the clear plastic lid over top of it. The familiar scratching sound starts pouring through the speakers, followed by the opening of *Singing Winds, Crying Beasts,* and I set the other Santana album next to the turntable for later.

"Turn it up, please, I hear Stef call from the kitchen, and it brings a smile to my face as I slowly turn the volume knob and amplify the music just shy of the point where intelligible conversation would be impossible. Once there, I turn toward his closet and see a series of black and grey ties draped over its handle. I pull the top one, examine it, and spot a grease stain near the bottom. A slightly darker tie sitting under it looks clean, though, so I swap the two, and stand before the mirror, popping the collar of my shirt, and threading the tie around my neck.

A memory of my Yaya flashes quickly; I'm getting ready for a middle school dance, and Yaya's teaching me how to tie a necktie properly.

"Why can't I just have a clip-on tie? I ask her.

"Your Pop-Pop would roll over in his grave, baby, she tells me, and then leans in very quietly, wary of my mother's presence. "The Mercier men have always known how to dress themselves. It's a matter of pride.

I finish the knot in front of Arturo's mirror and look myself over. My shirt's tucked in, my pants don't have any wrinkles in them, and my belt matches my shoes. My tie is straightened, and my face still looks clean from shaving this morning. The loose curls sitting on top of my head don't look very styled, but anyone can get away with messy hair when they're dressed sharp, and Arturo's tie helps put me just over that line. When I walk back out into the kitchen, Stefania has chicken cooking in the pan.

"You're just in time, she says.

"In time for what? I ask.

"You remember those potatoes we had at your mother's? she asks, and she points to a bag of red potatoes sitting on the counter top. "They were just *so* good, baby, I thought it'd be nice if you could make them again.

I'm caught in a weird place. It turns me on the way that she calls me *baby,* and there's always been something appealing about being in a kitchen with her, but then there's the issue of her brother.

"I don't know, I tell her, and I don't try to hide the doubt in my voice. "Isn't your brother supposed to be a cook or something?

"Yeah, she says, "but the idea is for dinner to be ready by the time he gets home. Otherwise, we're not eating at a decent hour, and I'm starting to feel pretty hungry.

"Right, I say, "but what about...

Stef cuts me off, saying "Look, Jimi, while turning away from the pan to give me her complete attention. There's a knife in her hand, and something forceful about the way she holds it. "Do *I* like your potatoes? she asks.

"I guess so, I answer.

"Then I guess that better be good enough for you, she tells me, and motions toward the bag of potatoes with her knife. "You just do what you do and don't be worried about whether or not my brother likes you. Now, go make me some potatoes.

"Yes, ma'am, I tell her, and I walk toward the bag of potatoes, ready to do work.

***

Dinner is ready by the time *Abraxas* finishes spinning; the record gets flipped while the potatoes are in the oven. I finish setting the table, and Stef is ready to plate all of the food, when she turns to me with a wide-eyed look and says, "*Shit!*

"What? I ask her.

"I was going to ask you to run out and get a bottle of wine to go with our dinner, she says.

"We don't really need wine, do we? I ask her, hoping that she'll demure. The food smells really good, and I don't want to leave her place. Besides that, I feel like if I'm in the room when Arturo shows up, I'll feel confident and in control. If I leave and he shows up, it'll be like walking into a conversation, and I won't know if they've been talking about me or not. I don't know why I should feel paranoid about such a thing like that, but I do, and I can't help it.

"Wine helps make the meal, Stef says, simply. "There's a liquor store just up the street. If you hurry, you can be there and back in no time.

"Alright, I tell her, "But I don't know anything about wine.

"That's okay, she says, "I know exactly what I want you to get. Look for a white wine called *Albarino.* If they don't have that, look for *Torrontes.* I'll text you the full names so that you won't forget, and she gets out her phone, punching the screen vigorously for a few seconds before pocketing it. A beeping sound comes from my phone, letting me know that her text has come through, and she smiles at me. Her teeth look perfect, and her lips have a shine to them, like she's just recently put on some balm. It's the kind of smile that I feel can get me to do anything, and suddenly I don't know what was making me feel some kind of way about leaving in the first place. Suppose her brother does show up. What could she possibly have to say about me that's bad?

"Give me just a minute, I tell her. "And if Arturo gets here before I get back, and he wants some kind of beer or something, just give me a text or call, and I'll pick it up.

"That's so sweet of you, Stef says, and it makes me smile. When I close the door behind me, however, I become immediately aware of my surroundings, and an anxious feeling sets in. I've been around these apartments before. How long before I'm recognized by some chick who feels like she's been jilted? The thought makes my feet move quickly to my car, and I'm in and driving before I even have my seat belt buckled.

When I get to the store, I start to tell myself to relax. How petty are people going to be? It's not like there's an army of women out to sabotage me or anything. They've all probably moved on to something more meaningful, like I have.

Inside, I walk back over to the wine section and I scan through the bottles, getting lost, before a guy working there tells me they're organized by country. I read off the label from my text message to him, and he tells me I need to go to the Spain section, and so I walk over there, and sure enough, the bottle I'm looking for is standing out there, waiting to be picked up.

"Easy enough, I tell myself, and I get in line behind a fat man wearing camouflage, and he's got wiry facial hair that he's trying to pass off as a beard; it just looks long and patchy, and only succeeds in making him look kind of dirty. The cashier, who is brown-skinned and looks like absolutely bored with the job, rings up the man's case of beer and tells him the cost in a very thick Indian accent.

"That will be fourteen dollars and seven cents, sir.

"Fuck you just say to me? the fat man asks. "Speak fuckin' *English,* will ya?

Even though I'm not the one who says it, I feel a hot flash of shame sweep over me, and I grit my teeth and cast my eyes downward, not wanting to look up at what unfolds. The cashier, though, acts like he's been down this road before, and doesn't flinch at any of these ugly words.

"Fourteen dollars and seven cents. Please. He speaks slowly when he says this, enunciating the words through his foreign tongue, and the fat man grunts at him in response, tossing some crumpled bills on the counter with a nickel that nearly bounces off when it lands. His thick fingers fish into a bowl of loose pennies, and he takes two out, tossing them in with the nickel.

“Get out of our country if you're not gonna learn the language, he says, and grabs his case of beer, angrily marching out of the store.

The cashier takes a deep breath, scoops the money into hand and puts it into the register. When I step up with my bottle of wine, he gives me the same exact look that he gave the fat man; blank and emotionless.

“That was seriously messed up what that guy just said to you, I tell him as I set the bottle of wine on the counter top. It's like I feel the need to apologize to him on behalf of the rest of world. “I'm sorry you had to deal with that.

“This is okay, the cashier says, but his look doesn't flicker. He scans the bottle of wine, and very calmly states, “That will be fifteen twenty-six. I quietly get out a twenty dollar bill, and when he gives me my change, I drop the four pennies into the dish of loose change.

“I hope your day gets better, I tell him as I grab the bottle of wine that he's placed in its slender brown bag. “Not everybody is that ugly.

“Thank you, sir, he says, expressionless. “You have a good day, too.

When I get into my car, I place the bottle of wine on the passenger seat, and slip out of the liquor store parking lot faster than most; faster to get away from a bad scene, and faster toward one with a little more promise. The drive is quick, and within five minutes, I'm back in front of Stefania's place, only now I'm parking behind a little red truck that looks old, sits low to the ground, and is slightly rusting out in the back. When I get out of the car with the wine in hand, I walk around the driver's side of the truck and peek into the cab. What looks like a balled up black apron is sitting on the far side of the seat, and my guess is that Arturo has made it back before me.

“Be cool, Jimi, I tell myself. “Stef likes you. Her brother will, too.

The door opens as I'm approaching the walkway, and a short, slender young man is standing in its frame. I can hear the *Abraxas* album is spinning again, and *Black Magic Woman* is just starting to play, or maybe it's mid-way through the song; I can't tell. I'm busy taking in Arturo's features, and I'm struck by the idea that I've seen him somewhere before. He has his eyes on his sister, smiling, and as he turns to look at me, our eyes lock, and the smile drains away from his face.

Something is making my palms start to sweat. "Hey, man," I say to him, and my throat feels like it's drying out. "My name is Jimi."

"I know who the *fuck* you are," he says, and his voice is cold and low. He turns to his sister. "Seriously, Stef? This is the *vato* you're seeing?"

He turns back to me and starts walking forward, and I can see his hands balling themselves up into two tight fists. "This fucking *pendejo*," he mutters, and I realize now very quickly where I've seen him before.

Arturo is a waiter at *Che's Diner*. He's seen the Breakfast Test.

"Relax man," I say, "Let me explain," but it's too late. Arturo is power walking toward me, and his fists are swinging like small pendulums, until he raises up his left and throws it forward.

I've been in a few fights before, enough to know that you have to put up a cover. The bottle of wine slips out of my hand, and falls to the concrete, shattering inside its bag. I try to bring my hands up to my face, and tuck my elbows in, but this is all happening way too fast. My cover's not strong enough. Arturo's left jab comes speeding in, breaks through my two hands, and connects directly with my chin. His right comes swinging upward and my jaw snaps shut with my teeth coming down on my tongue, drawing a sharp pain and some blood with it. I stumble and drop backwards. The back of my head smacks the cement, and the world around me starts to get fuzzy.

It's a powerful two-punch combo, but it's not enough to

satisfy Arturo. He's standing over me, yanking me up by *his* tie, and his right fist is hammering down. Stefania is rushing out of the house and pulling her brother away, but he lands one last punch that hooks around my arms and nails me on my left temple, and I am gone.

Nine: Mutual

When I open my eyes, I'm vaguely aware of a few things. I know that I'm on the ground outside, and I know that I must be at Stefania's place, because this concrete walk way I'm lying on is familiar to me, and Stef is holding my hand. She keeps telling me not to move, but I've got a headache and I want a glass of water. When I try to tell her this, a small groan gets stuck in my throat. I feel something warm trickling down the left side of my face, dripping into my ear.

"Cuando regrese, es mejor que no este aqui."

I have no idea what he's saying, but it sounds like Arturo's voice. When Stef replies, she sounds hurt and angry, and she squeezes my hand gently.

"Qué demonias te pasa?" she yells back at him.

"El es el problema, no yo." I hear a car door open. My vision is starting to clear up, too. The sky above looks overcast.

"El es mi novio!" she says.

"Es un perro. No voy hablar de eso aqui." The car door slams shut. An engine starts. I'm vaguely aware that the conversation was about me, but not meant for me. High school Spanish has failed me. I slowly prop myself up on my elbows, and when I do, the warmth that was going into my ear now seeps down into my eye, and it stings.

"You guys speak so fast," I mutter, "I can't hardly understand what you're saying."

"What?" says Stefania, and she sounds panicked, like she can't make sense of it either. "That was nothing. Don't get up too fast."

"Doesn't *perro* mean *dog*? It's like the only word I caught..." I tell her, still working my way to my feet. At this point, Stefania is helping me up, her arm under my own.

"Jesus Christ, Jimi, never mind the language," she tells me, exasperated. "Let's get you inside and cleaned up."

"Cleaned up? I ask her, and when I look down to check myself out, a drop of blood falls from my face and stains the bottom of Arturo's tie. In that moment, it all comes back to me, and I am overcome by an immediate sense of fear.

"Did your brother call me a dog? I ask her as we walk into her apartment.

"Oh my God, yes, she replies and her frustration is clear. "He also split your fucking eyebrow open. Can we focus on that for a second? Her voice starts to break, and I immediately go quiet as she leads me to the chair where I would've sat for dinner. Without saying another word, she heads to the bathroom to grab a first aid kit, and for the briefest moment, I am left by myself to take in everything that happened.

Arturo called me a dog. He knows about the Breakfast Test. He's going to tell Stefania. Stefania is going to leave me. I have to get out of here.

I'm patting my pockets but feel nothing familiar when Stef walks back into the room, holding a bottle of rubbing alcohol and cotton balls in one hand and some butterfly bandages in the other.

"Where are my keys? I ask her.

"They probably fell out of your pocket when you hit the ground, she tells me. "Be still.

She straddles me on the chair so that I won't be able to get up, and rests the first aid stuff in her lap. She opens the bottle of alcohol, pours some on the cotton, and starts swabbing the side of my eye. When I try to pull away, she grabs me firmly by the chin with her free hand.

"Don't move, she says. "He split your eyebrow open.

A flashback of Arturo's stiff punches landing resurfaces, and my sense of dread only deepens. I can feel my palms starting to sweat. I weigh my options, and if I'm going to survive this situation, I convince myself that my best bet is to just stay quiet and let her finish cleaning me up. Once she uses a dry cotton ball to dry the skin around my cut, she gets two of the butterfly bandages to hold things together.

"This will have to do for now," she says, and just when I expect her to start asking about why Arturo would hit me, she flashes a light in my eyes, instead.

"What are you doing?" I ask her.

"I'm checking for concussion," she says, and I'm amazed at how she's switched from nearly crying to professional-mode. There is no tone in her voice, and it's all business, with the exception that she's straddling me in her dining room instead of standing by my bedside at a hospital.

When she is done, I ask her quietly to get up off of me, and I begin the process of exchanging my shame for anger. The complete sensation of every punch is with me now, and it feels like parts of my cheek are starting to swell. It's one thing to get your ass kicked, and it's another thing to get your ass kicked in front of your girl, but this is something entirely different from both of those things. How do I explain myself? How do I look her in the eye? How do I get out of here?

"Talk to me, Jimi," Stef says, and she still has control over her emotions, like she's trying to keep an open mind about everything that just happened, but her own sense of panic is starting to creep in, and I know I can't do anything about hers without adding to mine.

"I'm just going to leave," I tell her, and I start to get up, unable to meet her gaze.

"No," she says, and she presses both hands to my chest to try to force me back into the chair, but I grab her wrists and pull them away from me, though I still can't help but keep my eyes cast downward.

"Look," I tell her, "I can't be here right now. I just got knocked out in front of your place by your brother, and I'm not going to do anything about that, because I care about you. I'm not trying to find him. I'm not trying to call up some friends. I'm not even trying to call the cops. Please, don't ask me to stay. I don't want to be here when he gets back."

And now, she breaks. Stef throws her arms around my neck and buries her face into my shoulder. “What the hell is happening right now?” she sobs, but I only peel her away from me, wordless, and walk out the door with her standing behind me, crying in a state of shock. When I close the front door, I ignore any and all sounds coming from inside the apartment. There’s no doubt the place has thin walls, and if someone comes calling because of what they hear, I don’t want to be around with a busted eye.

My keys are lying in the grass, just at the edge of the sidewalk. I pick them up, calmly move toward my car, get in, start the engine, and drive. It’s Sunday, and there’s always one place I can go.

***

If a mother’s initial reaction to her son showing up bloodied and bruised is supposed to be one of horror and compassion, there’s something comical about the way my mother handles things. When I pull up to her house, the sun is just starting to set, and she looks like she’s been doing some serious work in the front yard, using a claw to pull weeds from a freshly installed garden bed, throwing them into a large heap of roots and dirt. As I open the car door, she turns to acknowledge me and says, “Wasn’t expecting you today! I thought you were doing dinner at your girlfriend’s place?” When I come around the front and she catches full view of my face, her looks sag into an expression of complacency, and she sets aside her gardening tool and takes off her gloves.

“I guess you’ve got a story to tell me,” she says, and gets up from her spot on the grass and walks inside. “I’ll put on a pot of coffee. Wipe your feet or take off your shoes before you come in the house.”

When I get inside, I sit at the kitchen table, and it feels weird to think that just a week ago, I was sitting in the same spot with Stefania right beside me. The thought stings the back of my throat, and I feel like something inside of me is breaking. Mom keeps her back to me, busy with the coffee maker, and when she finally approaches the table, she places two cups down and takes the seat directly across from me.

“Let me see your hands,” she says.

I have not heard her ask me to do this since I was in school. I never got into very many fights, but when I did, Mom would look at my hands to judge how guilty I was. If there were more marks on my knuckles than on my face, she'd be pissed, and she'd tell me I must've started something to have all that action on my hands and not enough anywhere else.

Today, my hands tell a different story.

“Hmm,” she says, examining my fingers. “Not a mark to be seen. You didn't even try to defend yourself, did you?” She drops my hands back to the table and asks my very patiently, “So, do you want to tell me what happened?”

When I try to speak up, I can only muster a harsh whisper, and the stinging sensation in the back of my throat becomes more pronounced. “I think I screwed up, Mom,” I tell her, my voice starting to break. “Stef's brother thinks I'm some kind of player, and he doesn't want me to see his sister.”

“And he said so with his *fists*?” my mother asks, and I can hear a sharpness in her voice, like she's about to get defensive, and I can see all of the good will Stefania built up start to dissipate. I don't want things to become more complicated than they already are, but I don't know what to say, so I stay quiet. Mom stares at me hard, then says, “Well, are you going to call the cops and press charges?”

“Jesus, Ma,” I tell her, “Why in the hell would I want to do that?”

“Because you're an adult and that's how adults handle fist fights,” she tells me in a stern voice. “They certainly don't plot the next playground tussle or wait until the other guy's not looking...”

“I know that, Mom,” I cut her off, “I'm not calling the cops and nobody's getting jumped!”

“So what? You think you had this beating coming to you?”

she asks me, and the question is completely unexpected. It leaves me silent until I collect my thoughts. When I answer her, I can't raise my eyes up to meet hers, and I know I'm about to tell my mother a truth about myself that she probably won't want to hear.

"Arturo, I begin, choosing my words carefully, "Stef's brother, he works at this little café in the city. He's seen me go in a few times with a girl to get her breakfast, and every time I went, it was with a different girl.

"And this is why he thinks you're some kind of player or something? she asks.

"I didn't think it was enough to have some kind of rep, I counter, but there's a tone of guilt in my voice that I can't even mask.

Then my mother asks me, "Are you using protection? and I can't help but snap back in response, like it's the last thing I want to be talking about, all things considered.

"Oh my God, Ma, yes! How stupid do you think I am? I answer, but she comes back quick with the response.

"Son, if you're simple-minded enough to think you can just run around across the city, sleep around with a bunch of women, and not have it come back to bite you in the ass, then I think it's a fair question. Baltimore is a small place, but it's not *that* small. Rumors, diseases, and reputations can spread around pretty quickly. I swear to God, it's like you haven't grown up at all.

"It's not like it's a one-way street, I tell her, "It takes two people to sleep together, and I never got into anything that wasn't mutual.

"Oh hell, son, my mother laughs, but it's cold and mocking. "Nothing in life is mutual, not usually, and not by a long shot. She thinks about it for a second and then continues on, like she's really thinking about it. "*Definitely* nothing is casual... especially when you're sleeping with a woman. Always somebody ends up thinking more of what's going on than the other person next to them, and nobody seems to understand each other.

She takes a drink from her coffee cup, and I can see that she's measuring her words. I stay quiet, because it suddenly feels like I no longer have the right to speak for myself. My mother is presenting herself in a new light; a woman that's been scorned before.

"Everything we do has weight, Jimi," she continues. "If you didn't know that, you're about to find out. Never mind her brother and what he might have to think about you. Concentrate on what really matters now. Does Stef know you've got this reputation?"

My eyes drop again at the thought of it, and they fall on the spot of blood staining the bottom of Arturo's tie. There's an answer to the question that goes unspoken. If she doesn't know now, she'll know soon enough.

"What am I going to do, Mom?" I ask her, and I can hear how pathetic I sound.

"That all depends," she says. "How do you feel about her?"

"I think she's great," I answer, without hesitation. "I care a lot about her."

"Caring is all well and good," my mother replies, "but do you *love* her?"

The answer is struggling to make the leap off of the tip of my tongue. Part of me wants to deflect and avoid the question. It's barely been two months, if that, and that feels too soon to make those kinds of declarations. At the same time, we're also taking the kind of steps that people make when they're in a serious relationship. Would it be so terrible to call it for what it is?

"Yeah," I reply. "I think I love her."

"And that's your problem right there, son," she fires back, and the fierceness in her voice is unexpected. "You *think* you love her, but do you even know what love is? Be honest, Jimi. With all the running around you do, how can you expect a woman to trust you?"

The words hurt and enflame. I'm suddenly tired of feeling

bad about myself, and I have an ache to blame someone else. Anger begins to well up inside me, and before I can stop myself, I attack my mother with pent up feelings that I've only ever been vaguely aware of.

"You've got an awful lot of nerve to be talking about trust, I tell her. "You never had enough trust in you to keep a man in this house for five whole minutes. How are you gonna come at me like I'm supposed to know what it takes to make a relationship work? The only relationship *you* ever made work was with a bottle, and you don't even have *that* anymore.

It's deadly quiet in the room after that, and my mother's face turns to stone. She studies me, her face contorts, and I worry that she's going to start to cry. Then her face breaks, and she lets out a long laugh, and it makes her whole body shake. It's not a short, sarcastic thing, but a long, clear belly laugh with no sign of stopping. The longer she goes on laughing, the worse I start to feel.

"Oh, son! she says, collecting herself and catching her breath, "You don't have a clue.

And then she erupts in fresh laughter, like she just thought of what I said, and it makes her double up all over again.

"Stop it, I tell her, but it's half-hearted. My head is hanging low, and I can bring myself to look at her laugh at me.

"I'm sorry, she says, beginning to settle herself, "You'll have to excuse me if that's my response, but if you think for one *second* that you can make me feel guilty about my life and what I've done with it, you obviously don't even know *half* the story, and I can't be bothered by your opinion. I'm not ashamed of anything I've done, because I've had the decency to learn from my mistakes. You want to have this conversation one day, son, I will be more than happy to have it with you, but now might not be the time. You're the one with the black eye. Do you want to throw some more stones at your mother or do you want to do something about Stef?

I can't tell if I'm frustrated by her or by myself, and all I can think to say is, "Obviously I want to do something about Stef!

"Good, she tells me, and there's a steely edge to her voice that intimidates, like if I don't listen to what she has to say now, then I'll never be able to make things right. "Then you need to have an honest conversation with her, she says. "Go back there, and do it right now. Don't cower behind a phone call or a text message or whatever it is you might *want* to do. You go on and be a *man.* You knock on her door and lay all of your cards on the table. If your past is something you need to be ashamed of, then you tell her so, and ask for her forgiveness. If she gives you that forgiveness, that's when you might know something about what you're trying to call *a mutual thing.*

"What about Arturo? I ask her.

"What about him? she says. "Your grandmother and I learned how to get along. You and her brother can figure it out, especially if you both care for this woman. Judging by the condition of your face, I'd say that young man feels very passionately about his sister, especially considering that she might be all he's got with no parents.

The last part stings, and a whole new wave of shame crashes over me. I mull over my mother's words for a moment longer and I know that she's right. I have to fix this, and it can't wait another moment longer. It has to be done now, and in person. I take a deep breath and get up to leave. Mom doesn't follow me out the door. She stays behind, instead, staring into her cup of coffee.

Ten: For Keeps

When I leave my mother's place, the sun is just about set, and all that's left is the orange glow that comes right before nightfall. I'm already pushing it; I should've gone to bed an hour ago. My shift at the warehouse starts at midnight, and it would be nice to sleep for at least a couple of hours before I have to go in. Then again, judging from the way this whole situation has got me feeling, I doubt I'd be able to get any sleep anyway. Maybe it's just better to hope that I'm able to make it to work at all.

About half way to Stefania's place, I spot a supermarket that looks like it could be the kind to have a small section of flowers tucked near where they keep fresh vegetables and fruits. Most markets have a spot like that, anyway, so I pull in and grab a parking spot. Before I go in, I check myself out in the rear view mirror; it's not good.

The butterfly bandages look like they're barely holding on with the swelling in my eyebrow. Traces of dried blood that got missed in the initial clean up still linger on my face, and you can see it for what it is; a patch job that was done hastily before I had to run away with my tail between my legs. If they're going to give me sideways looks in the store though, so be it. Today will just have to be a day of judgement.

When I walk in, I immediately scan the aisles for where the produce is, and I see carts of vegetables under fluorescent lighting all the way to the left of the store. As quick as I can move without breaking into a run, I get to the other side of the store and scan the walls for where the flowers are kept. When I find them, I'm disappointed to see the size of the display. The selection is weak, and there are no red roses to be found. There are only bouquets of yellow available, which I grab and bag, because an attempt to give Stef flowers has to be better than no attempt at all.

The check-out guy is an older man who looks like he's retired from one job, and now this is what he does to make ends meet. He's overly friendly when he sees me approaching in the distance, and waves me over to his aisle with a big smile. “I gotcha over here, pal!” he says, and his attitude is upbeat to the point of being annoying, especially considering the circumstances.

Rather than lay the flowers down on the little conveyor belt, I hand them directly to the cashier, and he immediately cracks this corny joke. “For me? You shouldn’t have!” he chuckles, and starts looking for a price tag to scan. “You know,” he continues, “when you’re giving yellow flowers, they’re more for friendship, or an apology, right?” Then he looks up at me, sees my eyes, and his face goes slack.

“Thanks for the information,” I tell him, and I hand him ten bucks. Now he’s not so inclined to make eye contact. He puts the money in the register, hands me a fistful of coins in return, and half-heartedly asks me to have a nice day before I leave with the flowers in hand. God only knows what kind of story he puts together for a guy with a busted face buying flowers on a Sunday evening, but whatever it is, it probably won’t have much on the truth of the thing.

When I pull up to Stefania’s apartment, I can see Arturo’s ride parked out front, and I can feel my nerves start to spike. Part of me knows he’d be here when I came back to apologize, and my only hope is that he doesn’t try to hit me again, and that maybe cooler heads will prevail. I take a deep breath, get out of the car, and walk up to their door with the yellow roses in front of me like they’re some kind of shield. Before I can knock on the door, it opens, and Arturo is standing in door frame, menacingly.

I close my eyes, searching for peace, and I tell him, “I don’t have any beef with you, man. I feel like we got off on the wrong foot, and that’s my fault.”

When I open my eyes, he’s taken a step toward me, and he looks pissed. “*Wrong foot?*” he echoes. His right hand shoots forward, and his fingers jab me in my shoulder. I absorb his push and calmly step backwards. I have to show him that I don’t want to fight, and prove to Stefania that I’m not the guy he’s probably made me out to be.

"Let's just chill out, I tell him. "I'm seriously not trying to fight you. I came here to apologize for any misunderstanding and explain myself.

"Nothing's chill, *punta,* he says, and his hands become fists as he continues to walk toward me. "Especially between you and my sister. I know all about you, and I've asked around. You're sure as hell not coming anywhere near her ever again. His hand starts to rise up, like he's getting ready to swing on me. I should do something to defend myself, but instead, I stand my ground, clutch the flowers in my hands even tighter, and close my eyes, waiting for the blow that never comes.

"Arturo! ¿Qué crees que estás haciendo?"

I open my eyes to see Stefania, who looks just as angry as her brother, marching toward the open front door.

"Stay inside, Arturo barks, but he doesn't take his eyes off of me as he says it. "Fuck this guy if he thinks he can knock up my sister and then come around like everything's cool.

The words strike at me, and I feel like I'm losing oxygen. My knees start to weaken, and my hands fall to my side, with the flowers pointing precariously downward. *Knocked up.* Stefania's knocked up?

When Stef hears this, a new look enters her face, like she's just as shocked as I am, and she rushes out the door, and slaps Arturo hard across the back of his head.

"What the hell?! Arturo shouts, but he has to keep ducking as Stefania throws her hands around his face.

"Desde cuando eres mi padre tu? she screams at him, and her brother starts to cower toward the door. I am amazed at the way she has reduced her brother from over-protective to punk kid. *"Vuelve a la casa y no te métas.*

Arturo escapes his sister's blows, runs back inside, and then glares at me one more time before he slams the door behind him, leaving me outside with Stefania. Then the moment seems unnaturally quiet. We lock eyes and any anger that was in Stef's face drains away immediately when she's sees my expression, which has not changed since hearing the words come out of Arturo's mouth. Her eyes drift over to the roses hanging limply in my hand.

"Are those for me?" she asks, as if to break the ice.

I look down at the flowers, like I'm seeing them for the first time myself. "The guy at the cash register said they're supposed to be for when you're saying sorry to someone," I tell her, but it's like I'm talking absent-mindedly, and I'm not even there at all. "I was going to be smooth and tell you I bought them because they match the color of your dress, but really, these were the only flowers that they had."

Stefania looks down at herself and examines the yellow sundress with black polka dots, and it's like she's out of place with the world. The sky is too dark and her dress is too bright for this evening, and a happiness that seems to pour out of the dress is out of place in the context of the moment.

"Anyway," I continue, and I step forward and hand her the flowers, "These are for you."

She receives them, studies the bouquet for a moment, and then looks up at me again. "So are these just flowers, or is this an apology?"

"It's an apology," I say. "I'm guessing Arturo said some stuff about me..."

"Yeah, *stuff...*" she repeats.

"Look," I tell her, "Whatever planned thing I was going to say to you went out the window when I heard you were pregnant."

She hugs the flowers to her, but stays silent.

"Were you going to tell me?"

"Yes," she says, and her voice has a hitch in it, like any minute she could break down. "I was going to tell you at dinner today, but then Arturo came home, and when he saw you..."

"When did you know?" I ask, cutting her off, wanting to get to the heart of the thing.

She pauses for a moment, like she's collecting her thoughts.

Then she says, "I've never been car sick before. My first time throwing up during a car ride was on the way to your mother's house. Then, when I started talking about my parents, and I had to go to the bathroom because I was getting emotional about them... I've talked about my mom and dad a million times, and I've never come close to losing my cool, even with people that've been there and can relate. I was standing in your mother's bathroom, looking in the mirror, trying to fix myself up, and I was saying *What in the hell is wrong with me?* And then I had this thought, like a little tiny voice in the back of my head, and it was saying that maybe I was pregnant and that I should get it checked out. So on Monday, I bought a test, and tried it, and it was positive. Then on Tuesday, I bought three more, because false positives can happen...

"And all three of them came out positive? I ask her. She nods her head.

"Arturo walked in on me as I was reading the results, and I had these boxes everywhere, so it's not like I could deny it or cover it up or anything... He was excited when I first told him that I was bringing you over for dinner.

"Then he saw that it was me, I say, and her face cringes, like she's holding back some deep pain, but she nods her head again.

"Then he saw that it was you, she repeats, "And now I don't know what to make of anything anymore.

"I'm sorry, I tell her. It's the only thing I can think to say.

"Do you even know what you're sorry for? she asks me, and it's a question I didn't think about.

"No, I reply, "If I'm being honest.

She laughs slightly, but it's one of those bitter, quiet laughs, and she shakes her head. "Then why even bother with an apology if you're saying it just to say it.

"I'm not saying it just to say it, I tell her. "I'm saying it because I don't want to lose you.

"I'm sorry, she says, and the scorn in her voice is growing. "Did you say you don't want to *lose* me, or that you don't want to *use* me. I can't tell, *if I'm being honest.*”

I go quiet when she says this. Nothing is going the way that I thought it would. I don't know that I'm getting any credit for being here with the flowers, and I can feel myself getting angry for thinking that just the gesture itself would be enough to win Stefania over, especially without fully understanding the situation.

“Look,” I tell her, trying to find some kind of footing. “My head's kinda spinning with all this new information. I don't know how I'm supposed to take you being pregnant on top of your brother...”

“Forget about my brother, Jimi!” she yells. “Jesus Christ! There's something bigger going on than a stupid fist fight. Was any of this for real?”

“Yes!” I exclaim, “Yeah, I think this one's pretty real, don't you?”

“How do you know?” she asks. “What makes me so different from all the other girls you embarrassed over breakfast at my brother's work?”

And then I say it without thinking about it, like it comes through without touching any filter inside my brain: “Because we didn't fuck on the first night,” I tell her earnestly.

Her face turns to stone. “You are a pig, Jimi!” she yells, and she pulls the bouquet of flowers behind her ear and throws them forward, as hard as she can, into my face. The bundle smacks me in the nose before scattering everywhere, and Stefania starts marching back to her front door.

“Wait,” I plead, and I can't explain why, but I start to gather the flowers up off the ground like it's the most important thing I could be doing at that moment. “That's not what I meant by that. That came out all wrong! What I mean is that you're different.”

“I'm a *woman*,” Stefania snaps, turning her head toward me as she reaches the door. “I can't be all that different from the others that you've slept with.”

"Goddammit, Stef, would you just *stop,*" I yell, finally losing my cool. "You're not letting me explain anything."

When she hears me raise my voice, she reacts, but not in any way that I'd think she would. She doesn't try to match my voice, or flinch at my sudden outburst. Instead, she stops for a moment, like a strong sense of calm has taken hold of her, and when she addresses me again, her voice is very even.

"Tonight is not the night for your explanations, Jimi," she says. "You know, half the time, I feel like I'm playing mother to Arturo, and now..." She pauses, and looks down at her stomach. "I can't be in a relationship with someone who acts like a child," she continues. "I've got too many in my life as it is. I go to the doctor on Wednesday to find out officially whether or not I'm pregnant. You can call me then. In the meantime, if you really love me like you've been saying you do, just go away. Figure yourself out, and give me some space to think."

She says this, and then without hesitation, walks inside her apartment and closes the door behind her. I hear the faint click of a lock, and the light over the door shuts off, leaving me in the general darkness surrounding the front of her apartment. Unsure of what else to do, I place the yellow roses on the front step and walk back to my car.

I have felt this feeling before back in high school. I remember how I withdrew from everyone after being arrested, and how anything that was said about me by the kids in the hallway was like hearing about someone else who I didn't know or didn't exist to me. Back then, I just disengaged from the noise and threw myself into classwork. I became a machine, so single-minded in going to class to get work done that I ended up graduating middle of the pack instead of bottom of the barrel, where I had been. It was a feeling then, and it's coming back to me now.

Eleven: Hangdog

The drive back home is a slow one, and with the time that I have left, I decide it's best just to change into my warehouse clothes, grab a cup of coffee, and go to work early, where I won't have to think.

Sunday.

Monday.

Tuesday.

Wednesday.

I'll respect her wishes and wait until then to call. In the meantime, I know how to cancel out the rest of the noise going on inside my head. All it takes is going through the motions, lumping one box at a time, until the day's inventory is complete. The peace and quiet of working graveyard hours, counting items...

"HOUND DOG! WHO YOU BEEN MESSIN' UP, MY MAIN MAN?!"

All the way across the floor, late for work, bringing attention to my eye by shouting out the obvious, Harris Crockett comes strolling in, and he doesn't look so great himself. He's pale, and his face is unusually puffy. His energetic entrance belies the fact that he looks like he hasn't been sleeping. He has all the manic energy of a man ready to collapse, on the same level as the violent outbursts of a toddler before they're ready to fall asleep for the night.

The other guys on the floor watch him stroll in, and a few throw a look back my way, staring at my face and the butterfly bandages holding things together. Rather than address any of them, I turn away, shake my head, and get back to work. I've listened in on the breakroom conversations from time to time, and when the warehouse crew gets together, they can be as bad as a high school lunch room, which is why I've never been bothered by what they think. My face and Harris's reaction to it will probably make for a good conversation starter later on. The guys will speculate, but no one outside of Harris will come up to me and ask about it.

Mostly everyone stays out of everyone else's way when it's time to work, which is part of what makes the job so great. If you wanted to, you could work here for years and never get to know another guy by first name basis, what his politics are, or how he feels regarding the rest of the warehouse, all just by staying outside of the break room during your lunch shift. I've never been *that* distant, but I've never been too close to the other guys either, with the unfortunate exception of Harris, and that's only because you can't avoid someone when you're working side by side for an entire shift.

"Hot damn, he says, helping himself to a box filled with frozen vegetables. "That is seriously not a good look for you, dude. He chucks the box onto the pallet I've been loading up, and he nearly collapses all the work I'm doing.

"Harris, I tell him calmly, "Do not come into my space right now talking that shit and ruining my counts. You just put a product on the pallet that isn't even on my order sheet. Either come in here and act like you know what you're doing, or *get the fuck out.*

He stops and we locks eyes. The smile drops from his face, and his look turns to stone.

"I don't know who you think you're talking to, he tells me, and he takes a step forward.

I stand my ground. "I know exactly who I'm talking to, Harris. You haven't been on time for a shift in almost two weeks now, and when you do show up, I lose half my hours fixing your mistakes. You are literally the reason we end up back-logged with inventory, because you can't get shit done. No one else wants to work with you because of it, and I'm getting tired of being the only one willing to put up with you.

Now he acts hurt. "That's some bullshit, he says. "I thought we were boys.

A voice erupts from my chest. The cool demeanor that I've

been trying to keep locked down is gone, and the frustration with Harris, Arturo, and myself all comes pouring out. "This isn't a cubicle, Harris. We're not office buddies. We work in a fucking freezer. When you don't have your shit together, you put me at risk, *literally.* Not only are you fucking up my count when you take random product and put it on my pallet, but you just throw the shit on there, all haphazard. That's a case of frozen peas you just tossed my way. If it explodes, they might as well be frozen marbles that get scattered across the floor. That's a setup for a text book slip and fall, and I am not about to break my neck because you don't give a shit about this job.

The floor has stopped at this point. Everyone's looking at the two of us. Fist fights happen in the warehouse occasionally, and most people wouldn't mind seeing someone take a swing on Harris Crockett.

"So it's like *that?* he says, and I can tell by his tone of voice that he's not throwing any punches today. The only thing worse than faking like you're some kind of hard ass is when people find out that it's all an act. He knows this, and starts to work himself out of the corner that he backed himself into when he started jawing with me in the first place, which is fine by me. If there's one thing I'm certain about, it's that I need to hold onto this job and not lose it for putting Harris Crockett in line.

"It is what it is, I tell him, lowering my voice and finding my calm again. "If you don't like it, I don't know what to tell you, man. Take it up with Buck in the office.

He looks me up and down, his face contorts, and he raises his own voice now, in an effort to save face. "You're goddamn right I'm gonna go take it up with Buck! I don't need this shit. He turns on his heel and storms off toward management's office.

When I turn around to go back to my work, I hear someone call out from the other side of the floor. "Hell yeah, young blood, he says, "I been waiting for someone to tell that fool how it is.

I look over toward the direction of the voice and I see the lumping team of Blue Chapman and Migs Rodrigo. Blue's an old-timer, rebuilding his life after doing a twenty year stretch in prison. He typically carries a bible with him into the break room and tells us how lucky we are to be young and free. Migs is in his thirties and doesn't speak too much English. He was paired with Blue before I started work at the warehouse, because Blue became fluent in Spanish while doing time. The rumor is that Migs sends money back to a wife and kid, but can't visit them because of trouble with the law.

I nod at the both of them and Blue gives me a mild salute. A small grin slips over my face. It's the first good moment I've felt since getting punched out by Arturo, and I do everything I can to hold on to that moment, even after Harris comes back from Buck Johnson's office. All Harris does is work in silence and give me the occasional angry glare, but that's all. It actually makes the work that much easier for me.

***

The days cycle through in short order. I take as much overtime as they'll allow me, because I don't want to think about anything else, and time moves faster when I stay busy. After the blowout with Harris, I'm assigned a different lumping partner, a relative new-comer named Luke Conrad. He approaches me the day after Harris lodged his complaint with management.

"Buck says you're supposed to train me up, he says nervously, eying the bruising around the side of my face. It's a dark purple now, although it doesn't feel as bad as it did. He's small and stocky, like he can handle heavy items, but would have trouble reaching high places. He has a baby face that places him somewhere in his early twenties, but thinning hair that could make you think mid-thirties. Either way, he's looking at me like I'm supposed to be the authority, and it feels different.

"Where's Harris? I ask him. He shrugs his shoulders.

"I didn't hear anything about a guy named Harris. Buck just said a crock of shit was unloaded in deep freeze and that I was paired up with you on the dock.

"Wait, I ask, "he said *what?*

“He said a bunch of shit was unloaded in deep freeze...”

“Did he say a *bunch of shit* or a *crock of shit*?”

“Crock of shit. Why? Is that some inventory we've got to tackle later? I only brought the one pair of gloves...”

Part of me wants to laugh, but the rest of me knows better, and feels some sympathy for Harris. I've seen Buck do a move like this before. This isn't like doing a small stint of a few hours in deep freeze. This is a full eight hour shift. If Buck thinks there's a guy who is basically dead weight, and doesn't want to go through the hassle of firing him, he'll assign him deep freeze until he either straightens out or quits. The fact that Harris went to Buck and then came back on the floor hot-blooded and working while not a word gets mentioned my way tells me that Buck took sides, and it wasn't Harris's. Now I'm training a new guy and Harris is working in a zero degree locker. Sometimes things will change quickly when you don't expect them to.

“Don't worry about your gloves,” I tell him. “Tonight's work is going to keep us in the warm spots.”

“Warm spots?” he asks.

“Compared to deep freeze, twenty degrees feels like Spring. What's your name again?”

“Luke Conrad,” he says, and he sticks his gloved hand out toward me. I accept it and we shake hands briefly.

“Jimi Di Paola,” I reply. “It's a pretty easy job, once you figure out how to use the pallet jack and wrap the product. Beyond that, it's all about how bad you want it. The more product we move, the more we get paid. You trying to get paid?”

“Yes, sir!” he says, and I give him a cockeyed look.

“*Jimi* will do just fine, man. You don't have to call me *sir*. Let's get to it.”

The next couple of shifts pass in this fashion. I show Luke the ropes, and he's a pretty motivated guy, which makes life that much easier on me. He learns quick, and by Wednesday, he's just as good a partner as Harris Crockett ever was, if not better, which provides some kind of relief. When Wednesday comes around, my nerves get the best of me, and Luke's able to pick up some of the slack.

"Are you feeling okay? he asks me as we get into the first hour of our shift. "I know you said it feels like Spring on the dock, but I've never seen anyone sweat in a freezer before.

"Give it time, Luke, I tell him. "We all gotta sweat some time.

I can't help myself. My performance is dragging, because I keep checking my phone. Unless something's gone wrong, Stef should've had her appointment this morning. I called five times before going in to work, but it kept going straight to voice mail. I know it might be that her phone is dead, or she has it turned off or something, but I'm too cynical to believe any of that. I feel like she's ducking me.

When the end of the shift rolls around, most of the guys have been cut, including Luke. I ask Buck to let me stick around and sweep the dock for a quick clean up, and he gives me the extra hour. By the time I'm finished it's Thursday, six in the morning. If she's not up and accepting calls, then I won't have any choice but to go to her place and ask her what's going on face to face.

I clock out, slip into my car, grab the cell from out of my back pocket, and then I just sit there for a minute with my eyes closed, trying to find some center to the storm brewing inside my chest. I can't imagine what the sight must look like to the first shift guys that are coming into the warehouse, seeing a man just sitting in his car with his eyes shut tight, and the engine's not even started or anything. I allow myself to have that moment anyway, like I need it to imagine the possibilities of what's going to be said, and how I'm supposed to respond. I never really cared too much about what the future's going to look like, but now it's all I can think about.

I open my eyes and glance down at the screen. No new text messages, and no missed calls, but there is a notification. One new voice mail.

I punch in my passcode to open it up, and when the voice starts, I hit the speaker button to listen to it from the palm of my hand. The metallic voice announces *First Message,* and then I hear Stefania's voice come through.

"Hey Jimi, it's me. I'm sorry my phone's been off. I've just been sorting through a lot of stuff in my head..."

Her voice has a quality to it, like she's fighting back tears, and her tone is starting to get to me.

"...Anyway, I went to the doctor's office for the results of the blood test, and it's confirmed. I'm pregnant..."

Her voice pauses, and the weight of those two words comes down on me, causing my eyes to immediately fill with tears. It's an instinctive reaction, beyond my control, and a feeling wells up inside of me, but it's not a bad feeling. I can't explain it, and it's confusing as hell to me, but I feel the strongest sense of relief when she drops that news, like that's the outcome I've been hoping for this whole time. The feeling is short-lived, though, as her message plays on.

"...and just so we're clear, she continues, *"I'm keeping the baby. I don't know what I'm supposed to expect from you, Jimi, and I'm not going to force you to stick around, so I'm going to start off by not expecting anything out of you at all. You can call me if you want to, but I don't want to see you right now. I need time and I need space. I need to figure out what I'm doing with my life, and whether I'm even staying in Maryland after I graduate. You clearly need to figure out what's going on with yours. So, yeah, that's everything. Call me if you want. Or don't. I don't care right now."*

And then her voice disconnects, followed by an operator saying *End of new message...*

Before I start the car, I replay the message three more times, and then I save it to my inbox to listen to later. I want to call her, but I suddenly feel speechless. I'm scared, and I don't know what to say, so I return the phone to my back pocket.

***

When I drive back to my apartment, I don't bother with anything. I couldn't eat if I felt hungry, and I don't have the drive to do anything else, so I strip down, climb into bed, and I just lay there, waiting for sleep to come, but it never really does. I shift between intervals of staring at the ceiling and staring at my cell phone screen, working up the nerve to do something. Around 2 pm, I pull the trigger and dial Stefania. The phone rings four times, and just when I figure she's not going to answer, the line picks up and her voice comes through.

"Hello?

"Hey, I tell her, "I got your voicemail. It seems like an awkward way to start such a heavy conversation, but who knows what you're supposed to say in a situation like this?

"Yeah, she says. "I figured as much.

There's a pause in the conversation, and it's like neither one of us know exactly what to say in this situation, but I know what I've got on my mind, and I won't be able to go on until I put it out there. When I ask the question, it doesn't occur to me how stupid or immature it might sound, though, or how it might set her off.

"So, are you still mad at me? I ask her, and without meaning it, the tone makes it sound like I'm asking out of annoyance, when really I'm just nervous as hell to know what the truth might be.

"Are you fucking kidding me? she answers, and I can hear the disgust in her voice.

"So you *are* mad, I say, and I can't understand why I'm getting defensive, but I am. Half of me is dying to believe I've done nothing wrong, and the other half is dying for immediate forgiveness. Either way, it's impatience that's getting the better of me.

"What do you think, Jimi? she replies. "I'm furious!

"But why? I say and my voice rises as I start to lose control of my emotions. "It's not like I played you. We're in a relationship. I introduced you to my *mother.* I didn't treat you like the other girls I've been with.

I realize it's an admission of guilt. She knows what she knows, and I'm not denying anything. I really do believe, however, that Stefania is different and that she's the most serious I've ever been about someone, so it throws me off when she says otherwise.

"Oh, but I *am* like those other girls, Jimi. I am *exactly* like those other girls."

"What are you talking about?" I ask her, and she responds with fire in her voice.

"That day together, after the bachelorette party, when you helped me clean up my friend's place, what did you keep asking me to do?"

I'm silent now. I see what she's getting at.

"What did you *ask* me to do, Jimi? Answer me."

"I asked you out," I answer, but I know I'm trying to weasel out of the corner she's putting me in.

"You asked me out to *breakfast*. Café con leche? This nice little Cuban place you know? Is that ringing any bells for you?"

"So I asked you out to breakfast! It's not like we actually went!" I exclaim. "We didn't do any of the things I did with those other girls..."

"But we could have," she says, cutting me off. "You were going to take me out to the place where my *brother* works, and do what? Were you going to pretend to stick me with the bill after having paid for it, just to start a fight? Or were you going to wait until after you got into my pants..."

"Goddammit, Stef, stop it!" I yell into the phone. "You're not even letting me defend myself!"

"There's nothing to defend," she says, and then she hangs up, and I'm left lying in bed with my phone pressed to my ear, hoping that the sound of her disconnecting is a mistake, and that she hasn't given up on me. Reality sets in, and out of frustration, I throw the phone across the room and watch it hit the wall, bursting into pieces. I want that to be the end of it, and I want to be allowed to close my eyes and just stay in my bed and wallow, but I can't. I have to wake up for work. To do that, I need my phone's alarm.

I get up, collect the pieces, reassemble the battery and replace the backing, and inspect the screen, which only has a small fracture in the upper left corner. I turn it on, set the alarm, and plug it in to charge. Then I take a deep breath, lie back down on the bed, and stare at the ceiling until some form of sleep comes over me. When my phone goes off, I feel the worst I've ever felt in a very long time.

***

"See, what you need, Harris says to me, with his feet propped up and a hot cup of coffee resting on top of his belly, "is to get *laid*, you know what I'm sayin'?

It took until Friday for him to do it, but Harris is back on speaking terms with me. He's had deep freeze duty every shift he's come in, and he still comes in late, but he disappears into the coldest parts of the warehouse and doesn't complain to anyone about it. It's almost like a badge of honor for him, the same way a kid who gets suspended from school thinks that it makes him an automatic bad ass.

"And what makes you say all that? I ask him, holding my face over the steam coming off a bowl of hot noodles. The break room doesn't have too many people in it at the moment, since we all take different lunch shifts, and Harris feels free to talk about whatever he wants. Yesterday, he just wanted to talk about how much Buck sucks at managing the floor. Today, he wants to talk about my sex life. Luke is sitting at the table with us, but he stays silent, preferring to observe the conversation while he takes small bites from a turkey sandwich.

"You ain't got no *swagger*, man! Harris answers. "It's like you take one sucker punch to the face, and you wanna lay down and die.

"Shit, I say, "What do you know about my face or how I got this mark?

"All I know is what I see, Harris replies, putting his hands up. "Lately you've been looking more *hangdog* than Hound Dog. You might want to do something about that. Life's too short, man. He drains the rest of his coffee after he says this, throws the cup into a trash can, and walks out of the break room, leaving Luke and me to ourselves.

“If anyone knows about going out,” Luke mutters, breaking his silence, “it would be that guy.”

“What do you mean by that?” I ask him.

“I mean my wife’s a bartender at a place down in Fell’s Point, and I told her about some of the guys I’ve been working with. When I started talking about Harris Crockett, she said she knew him, that’s he’s been coming in on the weekends, and that he’s even tried to pick her up a few times.”

“What?” I say, with the lot of it being news to me. I’ve worked with Luke for almost a full week and I didn’t even know he was married. “How do you handle having lunch with a guy that you know has tried to pick up your wife?”

“I dunno,” Luke says, taking the final bite of his sandwich. “I mean, look at him. The only way he’s getting it is if he’s paying for it. Why should I have to worry?”

“That’s just sleazy, man,” I tell him. “That dude’s married and everything...”

“Harris Crockett is married?!” Luke asks.

“Yeah,” I say. “High school sweethearts, or something like that.”

“Got her while she was young and didn’t know any better,” he replies, and that makes me laugh. As we make our way back to work, though, the words start to sink in. Harris Crockett’s wife didn’t know any better. Stefania does. Maybe she might not ever forgive me. Maybe Harris is right, and that I just need to get out there, back to basics, and find one to help me get over the other. I could pick up a girl, take her back to my place, or even go to hers. I wouldn’t have to be picky, and I could even spin a pretty good story about my busted eye.

When I clock out for the day, I make the decision that I’m going out. I stop off at the apartment, grab five hours of sleep, and then get up to shower, shave, and get ready. Before I leave, I inspect myself in the mirror, and I search for traces of my old self, like it's been there for the past several weeks, waiting for me to come back to it. All I see is my black eye though, and I think about how I got it...

I shake off the feelings of guilt and reassure myself that things will fall back into place for me when I hit the scene and start talking to people. I'll find what I'm looking for then, and I won't even go to Baltimore to look for it. I'll hop in the car; take it out of the city and onto the highway. I'll drive long and head to one of those DC college bars, where no one will know me, and I can have a fresh back story. *I go to school at College Park, and I play for their Rugby team. Yeah, we do this thing where we shoot the boot when we screw up the lyrics to our songs. Law school is waiting for me when I'm done with my undergrad program. Until then, I'm just hanging out, having fun, and trying to meet some new people.*

It's nightfall by the time I get into the city and I find a parking spot after weaving in and out of all the traffic circles and traveling the diagonal one-ways. There's a lounge on 18th street that's all lit up, and very inviting. I scope the place out and make my way inside, ready to embrace whatever happens, but when I walk in, a weird feeling hits me, like I am a foreign man trying to make this place my own, but I don't understand the people or their language.

For one thing, this place is a little *too* hip. The walls are lined with velvet couches, and the bar top is surrounded by artsy looking stools that look like they're made to be appreciated by people's eyes instead of their asses, evident by the fact that there are more people standing next to empty ones than there are seated. The lighting in the place is this low neon color that makes people look exotic while they move around in the shadows, and the music pumping through the speakers is this awful techno shit that's just loud enough to make someone have to yell in order to be heard. For all of these terrible qualities, though, the place is packed, and with a solid mix of people, too; Black, White, Spanish, and Asian, all inter-mingling, and dressed like they've either got money or at least want to *look* like they do. I'm wearing designer jeans and a nice buttoned shirt, and I look out of place. I should just turn around and leave, but then I see her standing at the bar.

She's a short, slender girl, trying to get the bartender's attention, but she's getting boxed out by two guys who are hip to hip, waiting for their own drinks to come. I get a good look at her, and she's just the kind of cute that I normally go for; wearing hip hugging pants that shape her ass just so nicely, while her pale, bare midriff hovers just above, taut and smooth. A tight vest functions as her top, perfectly accentuating a nice small bosom; she's not flat chested, but she's doesn't look over-inflated, either, and the best part of her is the way her hair is done up to show off a long and slender neck, which typically drives me crazy about women. She looks frustrated, standing on tip toe to try and peak over the two guys' shoulders to catch a glimpse of the guy behind the counter, and this is when I make my move.

I cut across the floor, brush by the girl, and wedge myself in between the two guys joined at the hip. "My bad," I tell them, and then I slap the counter and yell to the bartender, "Ay yo, can I get a rum and cola for me, and..." I look at the girl and say, "What are you trying to order?"

"Malibu Bay Breeze?" she says, with a bashful smile on her face, like she doesn't want to be too much trouble. Already this is a good sign, and I know that I'm off to a good start.

"...and a Malibu for the lady. Please," I add, as an afterthought. I step away from the two guys at the bar, both of whom look pissed at me for having just walked into their personal space, and then turn my attention to the girl standing behind them. "Are you sitting somewhere?" I ask her. "If you want, I can wait for the drinks, and I'll bring yours over to you."

"Oh my God, that's so *nice*!" she says, and then points in the direction of the corner of the lounge. "I'll just be over there."

"By yourself?" I say, like that's some kind of crime, and she laughs.

"No," she tells me. "My friends are on the dance floor. I'm sitting out. It's not really my type of music."

"I feel that," I reply, and her smile widens. "I'll meet you in the corner with your drink when it comes up, and if you want, you can tell me about what music you *do* like.

"Maybe, she says, and I grin at the way she's switched to playing coy with me. It's about to get real flirtatious, really fast, which normally excites me. When she leaves and I turn back to the bar though, I'm left waiting next to the two guys joined at the hip, and reality sets in as I overhear their whole conversation:

"I'm telling you, bro, we oughta shoot up town. The Midnight Club's got the rave going on. There's gonna be tons of talent there. This place is beat.

"I don't know, dude, it's already getting pretty late...

"But that's exactly my point! Look how late it is, and all we got in this place are a bunch of chicks with tiny tits looking for free drinks without putting out...

"Aw, fuck it. Maybe you're right. This bartender's taking forever, anyway. Wanna just bail?

"Hell yeah, man. Midnight Club it is. There's probably a ton of chicks doing E right now that are just asking for it.

They turn and leave, clearing space at the bar. I take a seat on one of the stylishly uncomfortable stools and mull over their words. Without meaning for it to happen, everything they say I automatically apply to Stefania, like they were referring to her the whole time, and it starts to make my blood run thick. How would I handle it if I saw a guy like that calling her *the talent* and trying to pump drinks into her just for a shot at getting laid? And then I think about the cute girl in the corner of the room, waiting for me, and I get even angrier thinking about the whole situation; her part of it and my involvement as well. When the bartender arrives with the drinks, I hand him a twenty, tell him to keep the change, and I leave the rum and cola behind while I march the Malibu over to her. She looks up at me, completely bewildered when I slam the drink down on the table in front of her.

"Not that I would, I tell her sharply, "but you don't know me from anywhere around here. For all you know, I could've spiked your rum with all kinds of shit. Why are you taking free drinks from total strangers?"

"What the *fuck?*" she asks, "I thought you were just being *nice* to me, you fucking creep!"

"Nice guys don't typically come to bars," I shout over the music, still pulsating all around us. "If you had any sense, you'd know that."

Before I can listen to whatever she's got to say to that, I turn on my heel and walk back out of the lounge. The night is still young, but I suddenly feel sick to my stomach, sick over my situation, and sick of myself. When I find my car, I get out of DC as fast as I can and head back to my apartment.

My mind's gone into overdrive as I ask myself out loud, over and over again, the same question. "What the fuck are you *doing,* Jimi? What the fuck are you *doing?*" The interstate is at an odd hour of the night where it's relatively empty; everyone coming to DC has already come, and no one, save the few souls like myself, have found it's time to leave yet, so there's only a few of us speeding along the highway. The longer the road stretches before me, the heavier my foot gets on the pedal, until I'm doing nearly 100, watching my headlights punch through the darkness of the night while I weave in and out of the few cars that are cruising at the normal speed. It seems like with every extra mile I travel, the faster my heart rate seems to get, and pretty soon, it feels difficult to breathe. The stress of everything happening in my life starts to unfold, threatening to suffocate me, but it ends up being a sign on the highway that sends me over the edge.

Typically, the light up signs fixed to the overpasses checkering the interstate just display information about how many miles to the next exit and about how long it will take with traffic patterns, or where there's construction going on. Tonight, though, a display comes sailing out of the dark toward my speeding car, and the message hits me directly in the chest:

Work Zone Ahead: Slow Down and Save a Life Help a Father Get Home to Their Kid Tonight

Without warning, when the words come into focus and flash across my eyes, it's like all of the air gets sucked out of my lungs, and I'm gasping for breath. Instinctively, I pump the breaks, turn my hazard lights on, and pull over to the side of the road. My chest is racing and I'm starting to get lightheaded. I've seen people on television handle this sort of thing with a brown paper bag, but I don't have anything like that, so I lift my shirt over my mouth and try to steady my breathing. When my chest starts to slow down, I find my cell phone and dial Stefania. On the second ring, she picks up.

"Hello?

"I just want to talk to you for a second, please don't hang up, I say, fumbling for some sense of reason, knowing what I want to say without any idea of how to say it.

"Okay, she says, sounding tired. "I'm not hanging up.

"Good, I tell her, and then somewhat sheepishly, "Thank you.

"You're welcome, I guess, she replies. "Are you going to tell me why you called?

There's silence on the line, as I search for the words.

"Jimi? she asks, and then I blurt out the truth in its rawest form.

"I don't want to be a bad father, I tell her, and I know she can hear the panic in my voice, because I can hear it, too. "I never had one, and I don't even think I know how to *be* one, but I just know that I don't want to be a deadbeat. Like, what if I had a son, and he never got to know who his father was? That might kill me, Stef.

"So, what if you have a daughter? she asks me. It's a short and pointed question that I never stopped to think about.

"A son or a daughter, I stammer, "they deserve to have a father.

"Yes, I know that, and I'm glad you feel that way, Jimi, she replies, patiently. "But the question still stands. What if you have a daughter? Would you explain to her how to stay away from guys like you? If you had a son, would you teach him all of your tricks?

I'm left speechless. How does anyone respond to a thing like that? I feel like I'm being attacked, and I want to defend myself, but in the cold honestly of the moment, these are questions that I know I've asked myself, deep down inside.

"Do you even wonder why you did any of those things in the first place? she asks me after a pause, and I tell her the truth.

"I think I was doing it because I was angry.

"Who were you angry at? Women in general?

"I don't know, I answer, "Maybe. It's weird growing up with just a bunch of women barking at each other when they're not barking at you. My mom didn't even bring boyfriends home, and my Pop-Pop died when I was a kid, so it was like I didn't have anybody to talk to about stuff, and I just ended up getting angry about everything, and who the hell wants to be in a relationship when they just feel pissed off all the time?

"But you want to be with me? she asks, and her tone doesn't make it out like she's flattered or anything, but genuinely curious.

"Yeah, I tell her. "You're different.

The conversation could go further down this road. I want it to. All I need is for her to take it there, and we can hash this thing out on the side of the highway, and I can maybe even drive back to her place and see her, but she doesn't go for it. Instead, she comes out with something entirely different.

"I think you need to have this conversation with your mother.

"Not happening, I say, as just the thought of it gives me a sense of dread. Stefania isn't having it, though.

"Look, Jimi, she replies, "You want to work on making things right with me, then talk to your mother and sort out whatever issues it is you've been holding onto. I appreciate you calling me and telling me you want to be a father. It really does mean a lot to me. I wasn't lying when I said you need to figure yourself out, though, and this is part of that. Get your life together. When you do, then you can come and find me. Until then, good night.

She doesn't hang up on me after she says this. She waits until I say it back to her before disconnecting the call. When she does, I sit in the silence of my car on the side of the interstate, listening to sound of traffic breezing past my car, fast enough to cause it to sway. The rocking lulls me into a weird state of serenity while I think over the talk I had with Stefania. It wasn't the perfect conversation, and didn't end the way I wanted it to, but it was progress. I know what she wants me to do next. Now I just have to do it.

Twelve: Conversations

By the time I get back from DC, I'm surprised to see that it's not all that late at night. In fact, it's just barely past midnight, and I'm still primed to be up and active. The car ride had me thinking about everything that's been going on in my life, and a sort of after taste is left in my mouth from the conversation that I had with Stefania. It isn't a bad taste or anything, though. It's like I feel energized by it, the more I think about it. For one thing, she didn't ignore the phone call, which means she can't *completely* hate me. She might be pissed off, but the end of the conversation has me caught up in a lot of hopeful feelings, and there are other thoughts, besides that.

When I walk in through the front door, a sudden urge takes hold of me and I turn on every light in my apartment, so that I can check out every room. Since the day I moved in, I've only ever viewed my place as somewhere to crash, and I can't recall ever feeling like I would call it my *home*. It always struck me as having a transient sort of vibe, like I could up and leave at a moment's notice. Now though, I really want to get to know the place, stare at the walls and the carpet, and study the grout in the bathroom. I want to breathe in the air deeply and investigate any foul scents that linger there, and I want to turn on all of the ceiling fans to scrutinize the particles of dust that are thrown from the spinning blades. I want to move furniture and the refrigerator, and check the corners for rat shit and rodents. I want to size up the entirety of the apartment, and determine if it's livable.

By three in the morning, I'm in my kitchen, sweating on my hands and knees, stripped down to my underwear, and scrubbing the floor. By five o'clock, I'm taking down all of the posters tacked up to the wall that look like they belong in a frat boy's room; chicks in their panties making out with each other, or posing on the beach in tiny bikinis. When the hour reaches seven, I figure it's late enough in the morning that I can run a vacuum without pissing off my neighbors, and I take care of business. A little after ten, the apartment is as clean as the day that I first moved in, and I have a list of new projects that I want to accomplish, preferably within the next six months. For now, though, it will have to serve as a start, and so I get dressed and call my mother to see if she's ready to visit. Suddenly, everything has a sense of urgency now, like I want to change immediately, and move as quickly as possible into the future.

"Hey, Jimi, my mother says when she answers. She sounds cheerful, like it's already been a good day for her, even though it's only just beginning.

"You cool to have an early visit today? I ask her, and she makes a noise like someone who just remembered something they didn't even know they had forgotten.

"Oh shoot, she says, "I meant to tell you I was going to be out today. I'm joining some of my ladies for yoga in the park...

"Yoga in the park? I say like I'm disappointed, but she doesn't catch that in my tone, and mistakes it for curiosity.

"Yeah, it's this thing they do on Sunday afternoons in Patterson Park, she explains. "I'm getting together with the same girls that helped me with my house projects. We're going to go stretch for an hour and then grab some lunch. I might not be back to the house before your typical bed time. Are you going in later tonight?

"That's the plan, I tell her. "Look, if it's all the same to you, could you skip yoga today? I *really* need to talk to you, in person.

"Ha! she says, and I can tell she's getting ready to wind up and lay some great truth on me. "With the number of years I skipped out on doing things just to accommodate *your* schedule? I don't think so, Jimi! I made a date with my girlfriends, and I intend to keep it. I know you've got a lot going on, but I've got a life, too. If you need to talk to me that badly, you can meet me at the park and do some yoga with me and the girls. If not, it'll just have to wait.

"Well, what time does it start? I ask her, frustrated.

"One o'clock," she says, and there's a firmness to her voice like she's telling me she doesn't plan to budge on the subject.

"Fine," I reply. "I'll swing by the park at a quarter to two. We can talk then, before you have to go running off to lunch, if it's not too much trouble for your busy schedule."

My mother ignores my sarcasm and just fires back, "You mean you aren't going to come to yoga yourself and give it a try?"

"Why, so I can have some hippie tell me to focus on my breathing while I avoid stepping on the used needles that are probably littered all over the ground out there? Thanks, but no thanks."

"Suit yourself, Jimi," she says, and much like the sarcasm, she pays no heed to my cynicism. Then she adds, cryptically, "You're never going to be able to change if you don't open yourself up to new experiences, son." Before I can ask her what she means by that, she hangs up the phone.

***

When I arrive at the park, it's ten minutes until 2pm, and I'm lucky to find an empty spot on one of the side streets. The park is big however, and when I start to walk through the area, I feel like kicking myself for not asking my mother where exactly her group was going to be. I try calling her, but it goes straight to voicemail, which makes sense, considering what she's doing. I doubt they let you have your phone right next to you when you're trying to achieve a sense of unity and oneness with the universe, or whatever it is you're supposed to be doing when you go to yoga at the park. I shoot her a text to let me know where she's at when she gets finished, but in the meantime, I figure I can kill a few minutes by just walking around to see if I can't stumble onto their group on my own.

The weather is actually pretty great outside, and a lot of people are taking advantage of the day. I walk along the park's main footpath, keeping my eyes out for any small groups doing yoga, but all I can see are people walking their dogs, footballs being tossed around, and a large group of Spanish-looking guys playing soccer.

I can't remember the last time I went out to a place just to get some fresh air. It feels like the last few years have been mainly spent working and then going out to party, or some bar with a DJ that I can never really get all that into, interspersed with visits to my mother's place that are always more cursory than meaningful. It's a strange feeling to think that I may have been wasting years of my life and had not known it. Why didn't I go to dinner parties like the one that Stefania tried to plan out? Sure, Arturo saw me and everything went to shit, but it would've been nice if things hadn't gone down like that. Why didn't I even open myself up to the possibility of trying yoga, even if it would've been weird to be a grown man going to an exercise class with his mother?

You're never going to be able to change if you don't open yourself up to new experiences, son.

The park itself really is a nice area, and not at all like what I made it out to be on the phone. The grass isn't brown or dying, and there's no graveyard of dirty syringes lurking under your feet; people are happy, the plant life is lush and beautiful, and it makes me wonder something about myself. Is this a place I'd think to take a child? Would I have to be dragged out here by the hand, or would I have the sense to do it on my own? Isn't that what good fathers do? Do I even stand a chance?

"Jimi!

My attention snaps over to my mother's voice calling out to my left. She waves me over to a small group of about half a dozen women, all various ages, who are rolling up yoga mats and drinking bottles of water. Mom smiles when she sees me approach. She looks happy.

"Hey mom, I say as I approach her group of friends. When I get closer, I ask, "How you ladies doing today? A couple smile at me as they finish collecting their belongings, but no one really says anything. Mom grabs me by the elbow instead, and leads me away from them, with her mat rolled up and tucked underneath her arm.

"It's good to see you outside, she says. "I know you don't get to see the sunlight too much with the hours that you keep. It’s probably nice to know that it still exists.”

“Yeah,” I concede, “I was thinking something along those lines when I came out here, like I should be getting a little more sunshine in my life.”

“Well, we all need as much sunshine as we can get,” she replies. “Why don’t you walk me to my car so I can put away my things before lunch? I’m meeting the girls at a lunch spot where the soup is supposed to be really good.”

“That sounds really nice,” I tell her, then add, “Not that I’m asking for an invitation or anything.”

She laughs and tells me, “You’re not allowed to come to my lunch date, son. You’ve got your own life to take care of, don’t you?”

It hits me then that she’s probably more aware of my situation than I realize, and so I ask her, “How much do you know about what’s going on between me and Stefania?”

“Well, I don’t know if you know this,” she answers, “but Stef and I exchanged numbers when you brought her over a few weeks ago, and we’ve been texting each other sporadically. Initially, I did it so that I could be of some support for when she gets out of school. Regardless of whether or not you two were going to work out, I decided at dinner that I liked her, and that I wanted to see her be successful, so we’ve kept in touch ever since.”

“Do you guys ever talk on the phone?” I ask.

“Once or twice,” she says. “It’s probably not appropriate to tell someone over a text message that they’re going to be a *grandmother...*”

My heart sinks. It suddenly feels like I’ve walked into some kind of trap. My mother’s had time to think things through and prepare her own take on everything going on, and I can’t help but feel like this going to turn into some kind of attack.

“So when were you going to tell me that you knew about Stef?”

"Oh, son, she says, and her voice sounds so relaxed. "When I last saw you, her younger brother had just given you a black eye. It wasn't but a few days after that that I got a phone call about her pregnancy test. Was I supposed to come rushing to see what I could do, or are you glad that I gave you some space to process things and come talk to me when you were ready to talk?

"Is this why you wanted to meet at the park, so we could be out in public and I couldn't freak out? I ask her, somewhat defensively. It bothers me that she could've known this whole time and been so cool about everything.

"The world doesn't revolve around you, Jimi, my mother answers. "If you don't already know that, give yourself another six or seven months. You're gonna find out real quick just which way the Earth spins. I had a date with my friends. It wasn't a lie, for God's sake! It's called a coincidence, son.

I turn silent after that, thinking about what to say next as we walk closer to her car. I know the subject I want to hit on, but I'm unsure of the words, and I feel more and more anxious the closer we get to the roadside. Just when the car is in sight though, my mother turns slightly to the left and guides me to a bench at the edge of the park. She sits down and looks up at me expectantly.

"Get it off your chest, Jimi. Say what you need to say.

"How do you know I got something to say? I ask her.

"I told you, son. Stefania and I talk to each other. She told me about the conversation you had last night, and she told me that she suggested you talk to me to clear the air on some things. It wasn't a surprise to me when you said you needed to talk, so *talk*. We're all the way over here, away from everyone else, so you can even freak out if you have to.

I stare at her for a second, and then the question just pours out of me. "Why didn't you let me have a father?

"Your father was in jail; *is* in jail. You know why, she tells me firmly.

"Yeah, but why didn't you ever take me to see him? I ask her.

"The same reason you haven't gone to visit him since you've been able to drive," she answers. "You never *wanted* to see him. And why would you, anyway? He wasn't any kind of a father to you."

She's blunt, and the words strike me hard. I grab the empty seat next to my mother on the bench. She isn't wrong, either. It's not like I had made any attempt to visit him, or even ask how I could go about visiting him. I thought about him every now and again, sure, but in the same way someone thinks about a nearly mythical figure; beyond my mother and my Yaya's stories, his records collection was the only proof that he'd ever existed to me. It wasn't as though he'd ever tried to contact me, so why should I have had to bother with him? I really want that to be the end of it, too, but I know that it can't be.

"How am I supposed to be some kid's dad if I've never seen what one looks like in real life?"

"You had a father figure, Jimi," my mother says, like it's some well-known fact. "Your Pop-Pop Mercier was exactly what a father was supposed to be, and he would've done a great job being that man for you if he'd gotten to live longer, but he didn't. Lots of kids lose a parent early in life. It's a terrible thing when it happens, but they manage to grow up and become functional adults. Why should you be any different?"

I don't have anything to say to that. I could keep pressing the issue, but what would the point be? I don't know what kind of response I was looking for, but my mother can see on my face that I didn't hear what I wanted to hear.

"Let me ask you a question," my mother says.

"Go ahead," I tell her, and she can hear the defeat in my voice, but she presses on anyway.

"Why are you so angry at me?"

The question makes me instantly nervous, like I know we're going to rehash the last conversation we had at her kitchen table. I'd lost my cool with her, but she'd just laughed it off, and since then I'd hoped that that would be the end of that moment.

"I'm not *angry* at you, Mom, I try to tell her, but she cuts right through my words and gets to the point.

"We're not going to get anywhere lying to each other to spare feelings, son. And anyway, I'm not interested in carrying on another relationship where there's always tension hidden behind a polite smile. I had too much of that with your grandmother, and the only reason I dealt with it then was to protect you as best I could from any more ugliness than *you* already had to deal with. Let's just put it all out there, Jimi. Tell me why you're angry.

We're both quiet for a second after that, and a dozen thoughts run through my mind. Is an invitation to honesty ever really an honest invitation? Do I even know what I'm holding back? I think about it for a moment, and then it comes to me, and I tell my mother the truth of what I've been feeling for all of these years, and it's like a giant weight coming off of my chest.

"I'm angry at you, because you're the only one I know to be angry at. I never had a Dad to be pissed off at, so it's not like I could blame somebody that doesn't exist to me.

"So then you're blaming me for what, exactly? my mother asks, and when she does, there's still no anger or anything. She's completely at ease with the conversation, like she's been prepared for it for a long time now.

"I don't know, I tell her, honestly. "Everything, I guess. I blame you for being a single parent, for never having a man around for me to look up to, for being drunk half my life, for letting me fuck up so badly, and then actually doing something about it at the last minute. For constantly barking at me.

Mom absorbs all of these ideas, and she still looks collected. I'm ready for her to get defensive, but it never happens. Instead, she just asks another question.

"Do you feel better having told me all of that?

"Not really, I answer. "I mean, I don't go out of my way to feel like that. I've been trying hard not to, but it's just stuck with me.

“I know it,” she agrees. “I can see that by the way you’ve been treating some of these women.”

It stings, but what’s the use in objecting? She’s not wrong.

“Everyone screws up, though,” she continues, and she grabs my hand and holds it firmly, like I’m still her little boy, and she’s still handing down life lessons. “I made mistakes, and so did your father. I was in love with him, but he never wanted to change. He was being poisonous to me, and when he went off to jail, I was determined to not be one of those women who was going to waste their life waiting for their man to come home. I dated when you were young, but never brought anyone home, because it seemed like every man I dated wanted to tell me how to raise you, and what I was doing wrong. At the time, I know they probably meant well, but I was getting enough of that from your Yaya, and I just wasn’t in the mood to hear any of it. I ended up getting so angry, I just sort of swore off men. But then a person gets lonely and sad, and so yeah, I started drinking. I didn’t realize, though, that I had become just as poisonous to you as your father had been poisonous to me; not until after your Yaya died, anyway. When she passed, it was like losing the second parent in a two-parent system, and I suddenly realize how badly I needed to get my shit together. And so I did. It might’ve been too little too late, Jimi, but I did it, and I made sure you got through high school. Since then, I’ve been working on myself, little by little.”

There are tears welling up in my eyes, and when my mother sees them, she squeezes my hand gently, and pats my wrist. “I don’t tell these things to give you a sob story,” she says. “I only tell it to you so you understand your own situation. You get the ability to be poisonous honestly, from both sides of your family. I think we’ve reached a point where we’re not terribly poisonous to each other anymore, and I know how much you’ve been trying. I am grateful for the relationship we have today, especially when I think about how terribly your teenage years were for the both of us. The only advice I can give you now is that if you want to make things work for you and Stefania, just work hard and don’t be her poison. Understand?”

"I get you, Mom," I tell her, and fold my arms over her and hug her close to my chest. It's the closest I've ever felt to my mother.

***

Later that night, I go into work, and Buck Johnson is waiting for me by his office door.

"Jimi," he says to me, "My office. Need a moment of your time."

When I walk in, he tells me to close the door behind me, and asks me to take a seat. I get a strange flashback of being sent to the Principal's office in high school, but in those days, the administrator getting ready to hand out a lecture used to have a real ugly look on his face. Buck's got a half grin instead, like he's at a card game and he knows his hand is better than yours, and he's just waiting for you to fold.

"You a fan of tests?" he asks.

"Not really," I tell him. "It's one of the reasons I never went further in college. I never saw the point in them, so I never really studied all that hard."

"See now, that's just stinkin' thinkin'," Buck says, and chuckles. "Tests can come in all shapes and sizes. They don't need to be paper pencil. Could be a breathalyzer test. Could be a piss test. You ever take a piss test, Jimi?"

I tense up in a panic, suddenly worried about my job. "What the hell is this, Buck? You think I'm doing drugs or something?"

He holds the half grin of his for a full second, and then explodes in a fit of laughter.

"I'm just fuckin' with you!" he says, between bouts of laughs. He's nearly doubled over. "The look on your face," he stammers. "Oh, it was worth it."

I'm not laughing with him, but staring at him with a look of confusion, having no idea at all as to where any of this is going. Eventually his laughter subsides, and he clears his throat.

"Lighten up, Jimi," he says. "I like managers to have a sense of humor."

"Manager? I ask him.

"Well, yeah, he says. "I wasn't necessarily joking about the test part. That new guy that I paired you up with, Luke? That was your test. You passed.

"So wait, I say, still taking it all in, "What does all of that mean?

"It means you're going to be in charge of new hire training. I mean, we'll have to get you OSHA certified and all that good stuff, but the position comes with a decent pay raise, especially since our turnover rate is pretty high.

"But what about the old heads who've been here longer? I ask him. "What about Blue and Migs?

"Blue and Migs are lifers, Buck says. "They're content in what they're doing, so don't feel like you're taking anything away from them. Besides that fact, if you pull up job applications, you've got something that they don't.

"What's that? I say, and he gives me a look like he's both confused and angry.

"Your paperwork says you got an Associate's Degree in Business Administration! You do, don't you?

"Well, yeah, I answer, "But that was just two years at a community college...

"And it hasn't done anything for you since you graduated, Buck says. "Isn't it about time to put those credentials to work? Upper management likes it when we hire managers that have a degree. I looked your degree up online, and it says your degree applies to human resources management, right? You getting what I'm putting down, or do you need help connecting the dots?

"Well, damn Buck! I don't know what to say, I tell him.

"Say you'll take the damned job, he replies enthusiastically, and thrusts his hand out to shake on it.

"Right, I say, accepting his firm grasp. "Of course I'm gonna take the job.

"That's what I thought you'd say, he says. "Now let's get the paperwork on this thing done so we can schedule your training workshops, and more importantly, get your payroll updated. I want you to see your new hourly wage on your next paycheck.

I do, too. Two weeks later, the number looks a lot better with the five dollar hourly increase. Instead of celebrating with a trip to the bar, though, I go to the bank after work. When I finish talking to the person inside and sign all the paperwork, I go back out to my car, get out my cell phone. I want to text Stefania, but I hesitate, like I want to wait and build a better case for myself. Instead, I send a text out to my mother.

"Son or daughter, I write, "Doesn't matter to me. Just opened up a college account for my kid with the new manager money.

Two minutes later I get a text back.

"That's a good start, son.

Thirteen: Fathers

It takes me three weeks to work up the nerve to call Stefania again. In all of that time, I wait, hoping that she'll call me first, but it never happens. So instead, I keep the apartment clean and chip away at the list of projects to pass the time when I'm not at the warehouse. I paint the walls, replace the busted up blinds in the window sills, and even shampoo the carpet one weekend. When I'm not doing stuff like that, or working, I find myself going to the grocery store or someplace, but it's not to shop. Instead, I just go up and down the aisles where there's baby stuff, and I look at the price tags, running numbers in my head and figuring out how much money things might cost if this were to be a regular thing for me. Never once did I ever sit at a bar and imagine this part of the equation when I was talking up a woman, but here I am now.

When I'm finally ready to call, I decide I need a jumping off point, so I turn on all the lights in the apartment, and I take pictures of all the rooms, the new walls, and the clean carpet, and then I text them to her so that she can see how things have changed. Once I know she's received them, I call her up. She answers on the first ring.

"So I take it you got those pictures I sent you? I ask her.

"Yes, I did, she answers, and she sounds pleased. "I was just looking at them, actually. I like what you've done with the place.

"Want to come over and see for yourself? I say, but she demurs.

"Jimi, she replies, "I'm happy to see you doing some good things, but...

"But, what? I ask her.

"I just want to see if it sticks, she tells me. I'm not discouraged when she says this, though, and I come right back at her.

"Oh, it'll stick. Just you wait and see, I say.

"I *am* waiting, she replies, and the tone in her voice is closer to the playful sound it used to have before the dinner party happened. "Your mother told me about the job promotion. Good for you.

"Yeah, Mom said you two have been keeping in touch, I reply. I want to tell her about the savings account or at least ask if Mom has said anything, but I decide against it. If it comes up, she can be the one to ask about it. Instead, I ask her about her brother, and I can tell it's unexpected by the way she replies.

"He's calmed down some, she tells me. "I didn't speak to him for a week after everything went down, but eventually we talked about it. I think he feels like he's supposed to be the big bad *man of the house* or something, since our parents died, but I set him straight and told him we're always going to be brother and sister, and that makes us equals. He's never going to get to have a final say over who I choose to be with, but he has a right to feel the way that he does.

"So he still hates me, then? I ask.

"He doesn't *hate* you, Stef answers, thoughtfully. "I mean, he doesn't like you, like at all, but he doesn't *hate* you. I think I even caught him listening to the *Abraxas* album you left behind, quietly.

"Well that's gotta count for something, I say. "If it were me, I would've destroyed those records the first chance I got.

"Maybe, she tells me. "He at least has some respect for your taste in music, anyway. Besides that, it's not like he walks around all day talking about how he wants to kick your ass or anything. Lately he just talks about where he wants to go for his twenty-first birthday. You don't really come up all that often.

"That's better than any alternative I can think of, I reply. "Is he there now?

"No, he's picked up an extra shift over at the café.

"So, you're there all by yourself?

"You're *not* coming over, she says firmly, but I can only laugh lightly at her sincerity.

“Relax,” I say. “I’m not trying to come over. I was just going to say, when you get the chance, you should put on that first Santana album, listen to the second track, and think about me.”

“What’s the second track?” she asks.

“Evil Ways,” I tell her, then sing a few of the lines, “*Lord knows you’ve got to change, baby...*”

“So wait,” she cuts me off. “Are you saying that I need to change *my* evil ways?”

“Is that what you got out of that just now?” I ask her. “No, I’m saying the words to the song, the band is singing about how a lover needs to change their evil ways, and how it all can’t go on the way that it’s been. I just want you to know that I’m working on it. You can listen to that song and think about me changing.”

“So then in this situation you’re supposed to be my *lover*?” she says.

“Do you want me to be?” I reply.

“Good*bye*, Jimi!” she replies behind a small laugh, and before she can hang up the phone, I tell her that that didn’t sound like a *no*, and she laughs a little more before the line goes static. It’s progress measured in phone calls, but it’s progress nonetheless.

***

The week goes on, and I continue on with the new routine of going to work and then trying to find a different project to work on around my place, which at this point has me wondering about child safety locks, and if it would be too early to get started on that. Other than that, I stay dry and keep to myself.

As a matter of fact, I don’t think I’ve had a drink since the DC trip, and I don’t think I actually had a drink then, either. Really, I can’t even remember the last time I had a beer, though it’s not because I’m quitting drinking or anything like that. I just haven’t been out, because there hasn’t been a reason to go out. I stay out of trouble, and stay busy at work.

The warehouse is going smoother than I thought it would. I was convinced that the guys like Blue and Migs would be pissed off that I'm some kind of higher up now, but they're not. They tell me that it makes sense to them, that I'm young and ready to climb the ladder. Plus, if the new position means they've got me to blame for when a new guy doesn't know his ass from a hole in the ground, then they won't hesitate to let me know it.

When I show up for work on Friday, Buck's waiting for me again. He motions me into the office, asks me to shut the door, and then has me sit down.

"You settled in okay? he asks me when I take a seat. "No one's giving you a hard time or anything?

"Not really, I tell him. "Not like I thought they would anyway. Most people are cool with it from what I can tell.

"Good, good... Buck says, and then his eyes fall over to the phone sitting on his desk. "So tell me, Jimi. You ever hear the phrase '...and all other duties assigned'?

"Sure, I answer. "What, you need me to do a deep freeze shift?

"No, nothing like that, he replies, "But it does have something to do with that, in a way. Buck looks uncomfortable, and he shifts around in his chair a little nervously.

"What's the situation? I ask him, and he folds his big hands together and drops them on the desk, like he's about to get right to the point.

"It's Crockett, he answers. "We've been riding him pretty hard, having him doing multiple deep-freeze shifts. You've been here long enough, so you know the drill.

"Right, I say. "Trying to get him to *leave* so you don't have to go through the hassle of firing him.

"Between you and me, Buck says, leaning forward, "I would've been glad to have fired him. He just never did enough to warrant it. Sure, I could've nickel and dimed him with all kinds of write-ups, but then he'd probably fire back that I don't do that for everyone else. I know I don't run the tightest of ships around here, and that's the way I prefer it. Working in a freezer is a miserable job, and there's not much use in being so strict that you can't keep a crew together. Crockett, though..."

"You don't even have to say it, Buck," I tell him. "I know exactly what you mean."

"And that's just the situation I'm in right now!" Buck replies, and I look at him sideways, like I'm not sure where he's going with any of this.

"Crockett's missed the past three days," Buck continues. "I figure if it's a no-call, no-show, then he's probably quit, and good riddance! Then I get this voicemail when I come into work today..."

His hands unfold, and he presses a button on the phone system. The speaker clicks on, announces one saved message, and starts playing. It's Harris's wife.

"Hello, Mr. Johnson. This is Darlene Crockett, Harris Crockett's wife. I'm calling because I'm a little worried about my husband. Two days ago he said he was going out with a friend after work, somebody named Jimi, or Jamie, I think, and not to wait up. He hasn't been home since though, and I'm worried he's in trouble. I don't want to call the cops or anything for a false alarm though. Harris has done this once before, but I'm worried he's not coming back. If you could just talk to this Jimi person, or whatever his name is, and get back to me as soon as you can..."

Buck turns the message off this point, and it's a relief. By the end of the recording, it gets harder to understand what Crockett's wife is saying, because it sounds like she's crying.

"Buck," I tell him, putting my hands up in a plea of innocence, "I don't know anything about it. I've never gone out anywhere with Harris Crockett outside of work. I mean, not even to get a bite from the gas station on lunch break. You've got to believe me."

"I thought that part was bullshit," Buck replies. "However, I do figure that Crockett's been feeding his wife that line, anyway. Why he would, you'd be better able to say than I would. At first, I was worried it was an on the job accident, and I immediately searched the deep-freeze units, but there's no sign of him. I figure he's playing hooky, selling his wife a story that sounds believable, when really he's just going somewhere else for kicks.

The thought of Harris Crockett being able to get his kicks anywhere is enough to turn a stomach made of stone, but then the message has me thinking. "I think I got an idea where Harris might be, I say. "Is there any way you could call Luke Conrad into the office?

Without asking me why, Buck just picks up the phone, pressed a button, and speaks into the receiver, loud and clear, "Luke Conrad, you are wanted in the break room. Luke Conrad, to the break room. Then he puts the phone down, gets up from his chair, and motions me out his office and over to one of the empty tables by the vending machines. When Luke walks in, he's pale faced and panic stricken.

"Is everything okay? he asks, seeing the both of us sitting at the table waiting for him.

"Relax man, I tell him, "There's no reason to break a sweat. You don't even have to have a seat. I just need to ask you a quick question.

"Oh, thank God, man, he says. "I thought I was fired or something!

"No way, I answer, "You're all right. I just wanted to ask you about the conversation we had a few weeks ago. You remember when you were talking about how your wife saw Harris Crockett hanging out around the bars in Fell's Point?

"Yeah, I remember that, he replies.

"You wouldn't happen to know what bar that was, would you? Buck asks, picking up on the direction of the conversation. His rasping voice causes Luke to stand up a little straighter, almost like the military. It would be comical if the guy didn't still look like he was worried that he was about to get canned.

"You mean the place my wife works? She tends bar over at Dog's Ear, on Thames.

"That's all we needed, Buck says, and a look of confusion sweeps over Luke's face, which Buck promptly ignores. "Didn't mean to scare you, he continues. "Go on back to work.

When Luke leaves the break room, I turn my attention to Buck and ask him, “So that line about *all other duties assigned,* is that supposed to mean I have to go over to the Dog's Ear Tavern to try to hunt down Harris Crockett?”

“You don't mind, do you?” Buck asks. “It's not too often that you have a manager tell you to kick rocks for the day and go to the bar, right? We'll just make it an unofficial, informal thing. You'll stay on the clock for your shift – no overtime of course – and just scope out the scene. If he's there, you say something to him. I don't know. I'm just a sucker for these sorts of things, and I hate to hear a wife that upset. Maybe you could talk some sense into him if he's hanging out at the place you think he is. If he's not, we did our duty, and you'll call his wife and tell her to call the police to file a report if she needs to.”

“What do you mean *I'll* have to call his wife?” I ask. Buck just grins at me.

“Shit rolls downhill, Jimi. You didn't think a management spot would be all sunshine and giggles, did you?”

***

It's almost midnight by the time I find street parking and am able to navigate through the crowd of people looking for a good time in Fell's. Why Buck would choose to send me out at all, let alone on a Friday night is crazy enough by itself, but to make matters worse, I'm still wearing my insulated overalls that I use for the warehouse, and it is hot as Hell when you're trying to squeeze through everyone looking for a good time.

The line to get into the Dog's Ear isn't terrible, but it's long enough to get me irritated that I have to even be there in the first place. Once I get inside, it really feels like I'm on fire. This place has to be pushing the limits of some kind of fire code with the number of people they've stuffed in here, and I'm not interested in socializing with anyone. I'm pissed off and I have to find Harris Crockett. If I find him, I'll ask him what his problem is, and then I'll probably go back to work. I'm not interested in kicking any rocks or buying myself a drink on the company's dime. I just want to drive back to work, preferably with my head sticking out the window for any kind of breeze, do my job when I get there, and get on with my life in general.

Fortunately for me, Harris isn't all that hard to find. He's at the corner of the bar with a beer in one hand, while his free arm is wrapped around one of the most unfortunate looking women I have ever seen. She looks almost skeletal, especially standing next to Harris's ample body, and it wouldn't be surprising at all to learn that she's a meth addict. She leans in like she's going to nibble on Harris's earlobe, and it's about all I can stand to see, so I push forward through the various people standing around, and force my way to the bar top to get in Harris's free ear. As I approach, he catches sight of me, and erupts with a loud voice that makes the girl he's with cringe.

"Hound Dog! he hollers, *"HEY! It's a party now!* I can only roll my eyes when I hear him call out to me, and it takes me another minute to get close enough to lean in on him so I don't have to raise my voice over everyone else at the bar.

"Yo man, I tell him, "Who the fuck are you standing with right now, why are you at a bar when you should be at work, and why are you telling your wife that you and I have been going out, instead of you going home?

"Aw man, he replies, "Did that fat bitch call the warehouse to rat me the fuck out?

"Jesus Christ, Harris! I say, "What the fuck is wrong with you, man? If you aren't happy at home, that's one thing, but this isn't the way to deal with shit, and you certainly shouldn't be dragging my name into any of your shit. I don't need that kind of love...

"He don't NEED that kind of love!" Harris shouts to the rest of the bar, as though everyone was paying attention to our conversation, and I can feel my anger getting worse. "What you need, Jimi boy, he continues, "Is to lighten the fuck up and have a beer. I liked you better when you weren't acting like an uppity little bitch.

"Who the fuck are you calling uppity? I say, and I can hear the level of my voice rising, and now I know there are people starting to pay attention to us. The woman standing next to Harris senses trouble, and she detaches herself from him, turns around, and stumbles into the crowd, disappearing almost immediately.

"No one, mister manager, *sir*! he answers, and he sits up straight and gives me a mock salute. Now I've had it with his bull shit.

"You know what, I say, "I don't know what this is about, but it damn sure isn't gonna be about me, Harris. I snatch the beer out of his hand and throw it in a trash can tucked behind the bar. "Go home, I continue. "If you're not going to go to work, go home to your wife and kids, man. Stop being a piece of shit and go be someone's father.

"Fuck you, Houndog! he yells, and both of his hands come forward, connecting with my chest, and I fall backward into the crowd. The people standing directly behind me keep me propped up though, and they don't let me fall to the ground. At the same time, they're also not trying to stop Harris either, and he looks like he's winding up to try and kick my ass.

Without thinking about it, my right hand shoots forward, catching Harris in the chin just as he's pressing in on me, and his knees buckle. The rest of the bar reacts with loud whooping noises, which attracts the attention of the bouncers, who are remarkably quick. Before the fight can go any further, Harris and I are both being held up by two men built like professional body builders. They have each of us in a full nelson, with our arms dangling helplessly over our heads. People are turning to look at us as we're removed, especially since Harris is cussing the bouncer and telling everyone *I* started it. For my part, though, I'm just moving exactly the way I should with him, resigned to being thrown out of the bar and not struggling at all, which I think the bouncer picks up on, because as we get toward the door, his grip relaxes slightly and it stops feeling like my shoulders are going to pop out of their sockets.

Harris is the first one thrown out into the street, and just when I'm about to be next, the bouncer quickly releases his grip and stops short of the grand exit. Apparently, while Harris was getting tossed, another bouncer had come up and whispered something into this guy's ear, which gets me released.

"Sorry about that, the new bouncer says. "We didn't realize you were one of Arturo's buddies. He's in the room reserved in the back, if you'll just follow me, and you can rest assured that that guy will not be allowed back in here tonight.

Confused, I follow the bouncer, and let him lead me the way to a room marked private at the back of the bar, close to where Harris was sitting when I arrived, and where Arturo is apparently waiting for me, having called me one of his *buddies.*

Fourteen: Arturo

The private room might as well be its own separate club with how big it is, and especially with the way the sounds of the main bar don't bleed into the room when the door is closed behind me. Whereas everyone in the larger part of the Dog's Ear is listening to a DJ spin some techno remix of songs from the 80s, Shakira is what's pumping through the speakers for Arturo's party. The lights are low and a mirrored ball is spinning from the center of the room, throwing flecks of light on the forty or fifty people either slowing walking around in their social circles, dancing on the floor, or leaning on the bar to the far left of the room. To the right are various tables and booths, and in the back corner is a small table with a few people sitting in the shadows. I look off in that direction, expecting to see Arturo surrounded by a few of his closest friends; instead, I feel a tap on my shoulder, and I turn around to see Stefania's brother with two beers in his hand, standing behind me, ready to offer one up.

"Hey man," I tell him, reflexively putting my palms up in defense. "I'm not looking for any trouble..."

"Me neither," he says calmly, still offering the beer, patiently waiting for me to accept it. I take it, cautiously, but he doesn't react to this. Instead, he motions over to one of the tables by the side of the room and says, "Come on. Let's talk about some things."

A part of me doesn't want to, worried that this is all one big set up. It doesn't help that as I'm walking behind Arturo to the table, several of his friends keep looking up at me with either ugly or confused looks. It probably doesn't help that I'm still wearing my insulated overalls and have no business being inside someone's birthday party, considering the way everyone else is dressed, but I'm paranoid, and worried that it might be more than just a dress code violation that's attracting these kinds of looks. Still, when we get to the table and each grab a seat, I remember how my mom said she and Yaya found a way to make things work. I know what I want, and I know what I've got to do to make it work. Making peace with Arturo had to be a part of that sometime; if a coincidence is what it takes, then I might as well call it fate and dive into the conversation with as much strength as I can manage, starting with the opening words.

"Arturo, I say, sitting down, "Can I just tell you that I'm sorry about the terrible first impression I made on you? I know you saw me with those other women, and you're not wrong to think I'm an asshole.

"Yeah, Arturo concedes, looking down at the table and taking a sip of his beer, "you made it pretty easy to hate you.

"But you got to know, I continue, "I'm not interested in ever being that guy again, regardless of whether or not things work out between me and your sister. Not that I don't want to be with Stefania, though. Just the opposite, actually.

"I know, Arturo says, and he looks up at me like he's trying to study me. "I've noticed all the stuff you've been doing to try and work your way back.

"What do you mean? I ask him, and he grips his beer bottle with both hands, leans forward in his chair, and starts to explain.

"So a few days ago, I walked into my room, he says, "and I see my sister sitting on my bed, listening to one of the Santana albums you left behind, which I was fully intending to keep, by the way. I crack a smile when he says this, and he notices it before continuing on. "Anyway, there she is, sitting on my bed, looking like she's been crying, and I'm just ready to find you and kick your ass all over again, but I stop and ask her what's the matter? She says *nothing, it's just this stupid pregnancy,* but I know better and I press her a little more, and then she tells me all about *you.* She tells me about how you've been keeping in touch, fixing your place up, and how you got a promotion and shit at your job.

I listen quietly, wondering where this is going, as Arturo becomes more animated the deeper he gets into the story. One hand even breaks away from his bottle and starts emphasizing certain points, thrown about spasmodically at random intervals.

"Of course, I'm not trying to hear any of that," he continues, "because, and no offense now, but at the time I was like *fuck you,* because of the janky shit I saw you pull with the girls I seen you come in with at the café."

Just when I think I have no idea where this is going, he rounds to the point, and it's one of those moments where, again, having Harris Crockett in my life has somehow been a benefit to my personal relationships with other people.

"But then," he tells me, "I overheard that shit you said to the *cabron* at the bar, about how he needed to man the fuck up and be a father..."

"Wait," I ask, cutting him off. "I didn't even see you at the bar. When did you hear me say all that?"

"Ain't no bathrooms in here," Arturo explains, and on reflex, I look around to see if he's right. Sure enough, there aren't any other doors in the room beside the one we came in, with the exception of a Fire Exit all the way in the back. "See, I left to go take care of business," he says, "and when I came back, I spotted you at the bar. Now, I won't lie, I was walking over your way to tell you to find another place to drink, but when I got over your way, you were so into telling that dude about himself that it didn't look like you noticed me coming back from the bathroom. I ended up seeing the whole thing go down, and when you got snatched up, after hearing what you said, I realized I couldn't just let you get booted like that. My boy Manny's working the door to the private room tonight, so I asked him to step up for you, and said that it was a misunderstanding and all that stuff. So now here you are, instead of on your ass outside the bar."

"Well, thanks for that," I tell him. "I've been dropped on my ass enough as it is."

"Yeah, about that," Arturo says, but I hold up my hand and stop him before he can begin.

"Look man," I say, "You hitting me like that was a wake-up call. I'm ready for it to be water under the bridge if you are."

Now it's Arturo's turn to look confused. He cocks his head to the side, as if he wasn't sure he just heard what I said, so I double down.

"Seriously, man. Someone was gonna do it eventually, and besides that, I always kinda felt bad about the stuff I was doing, but I just kept lying to myself to try to justify acting like a scared punk. When I started seeing your sister, I was so nervous that she was gonna find out and not want to be with me, that that's when I realized just how wrong I'd been acting. It took me a long time to figure all that out and just admit to it, but it's out there now, and I'm working on being better. If it was gonna be anyone trying to throw hands with me, it might as well be you.

I take a long drink from my beer after saying this, and it really does feel like another set of weights has been taken off of me. I feel lighter, and a little more relaxed, especially now that I'm confident Arturo isn't ready to kill me or anything. If he and I can build a bridge, then I feel like I'm that much closer to getting back to Stefania.

Arturo is quiet for a second, sipping his own beer while he thinks about what I've just said, and then he shakes his head, and his eyes drop back down to the table again. "Nah, man, he tells me. "It still wasn't right. I got my sister trying to do her thing, with a nice dinner and all, not realizing what was at stake... It was wrong. I mean, Stef really had to set me straight. I was acting like a fool.

"My mother says it just meant that you cared a lot for her, which is why I didn't go running off to the police or anything, I say.

"Yeah, I actually appreciate you not being a little *puta* about all that, he replies, "but that still wasn't the right way to do business.

"So what do you say? We let bygones be bygones and I'll buy you a drink for your birthday? I say to him, and I extend my hand toward his. He accepts it, and we shake hands firmly. I suddenly feel a lot better about everything.

As we're walking to the bar, Arturo leans in on me and asks,

"Did you really ask my sister to listen to *Evil Ways* and think about you?"

"Yeah," I say, sheepishly, and he just laughs.

"You are corny as *hell*, man," he says.

Fifteen: Stefania

I don't spend much time at the Dog's Ear with Arturo. After I buy him a drink and finish my beer, he asks me if I'm sure I can't stay for one more, but I tell him that the guy getting tossed by the bouncer was actually a work-related thing, and I've got to go back to my shift. He gives me a nod, like he respects the fact that I'm dedicated to the job; it's one more shred of evidence that I'm not totally worth writing off. I shake his hand, wish him a happy birthday, and go back to my car. When I get back to the warehouse, I go right to Buck's office, and he gives me a wide grin as I walk through the door.

"Just couldn't knock off completely, could you?" he asks, and I shake my head as I grab the seat in front of his desk.

"No, you know I can't," I answer. "Besides, you might be a little short staffed after I tell you what went down."

I tell him the story, and Buck's mouth drops open when I tell him the part about getting him on the chin.

"And he just folded like a house of cards, huh?" he says, like he's been wondering what it would be like to punch Harris Crockett for some time. Then, as an afterthought, he adds, "You don't think he'll try to press charges on you or anything, do you?"

"I'm not nervous," I tell him. "I mean, he pushed me *first*, right? I have a right to defend myself. Besides that, he was drunk at a bar with his arm around what I'm pretty sure was a prostitute, when he was supposed to be at work. Don't you think he's got bigger things to worry about?"

"Yeah," Buck replies, but his voice drops a little when he says this, and he shifts around uncomfortably in his seat for a second before he picks up the phone on his desk. I sit quietly and watch as he moves a few papers around the pile that's in front of him, finds a small slip that he must've been looking for, and then punches in a number. A few seconds later, I hear a small voice from the receiver; I can't make out what's being said, but I can tell it's Harris's wife. Buck doesn't put it the phone on speaker, but keeps it a private conversation.

"Yes, hello," he rasps, "This is Buck Johnson. I got the message you left me and I wanted to call you back."

There's a slight pause. Buck's eyebrows raise up a bit.

"Oh, he did, did he? Well, I'm glad to hear he's made it home okay." He looks up at me and gives me a thumbs up, and then continues on with the conversation. "Well, yeah, I have to be honest with you, ma'am. The line he gave you about going out with one of my employees wasn't exactly accurate, though I did send Jimi down to where he thought your husband might be to try and talk some sense into him."

There's another pause, and Buck's eyes lower a bit.

"Naturally," he continues, "and I'm glad he's home now. Look, I hate to pile on to your situation, but you understand that as of now your husband has been terminated... I sympathize, I really do, but I've got a warehouse to run, and your husband will simply have to find a new place of employment. I'll mail the final paycheck... No, there won't be any need to come in... Yes, indeed, and I'm sorry for your troubles. Goodbye."

He hangs up the phone and lets out a deep breath. I didn't think firing Harris Crockett would be that stressful, but with the way Buck is, it looks like he'd rather have done anything else. When he looks up, he guesses at my reaction, and explains himself.

"Firing that Crock-o-shit wasn't the problem, Jimi," he tells me. "That's been coming for some time now. I just didn't realize I'd have to give the news to his wife..."

"Well," I reply, "she married him, right? It's not like she doesn't know what she's getting having Harris for a husband."

"Maybe," Buck says, thoughtfully. "Could be that I'm getting softer as I get older, but I've been down that road before, and I don't think it's fun for anyone."

"What road?" I ask him. "Were you lying about going to work and getting drunk at a bar instead?"

"Marital problems, Jimi, Buck replies, and he ignores my sarcasm with a wave of his hand. "You wouldn't understand. You're young and single.

"Yeah, but what's Harris Crockett's marriage got to do with you? I say. "He made his own problems.

"Look, Buck answers, and his eyes narrow on me, "Just because the guy is an asshole doesn't mean he won't get my sympathy. All relationships hit that one speed bump that makes you feel like you're gonna drive right off the road. Sometimes it happens early on, like with Harris, and sometimes it happens later in life, but when it does, it's scary. I was married for twenty five years before I found that bump and almost hit the guard rails myself. I mean it when I say I feel for *both* of them right now.

"What happened? I ask, leaning forward in my chair, totally interested in what Buck might say next. He leans back, puts his hands on top of his head, and lets out a big sigh, like it's painful just having to recite the details.

"Oh, our son was graduating from high school, Buck says, staring up at the ceiling while he tells the story. "Biggest day of his life, right? My wife's about seventy-two different kinds of excited for it, being that he's the only kid we've got, so she puts together a big party. We've got relatives driving up from Florida, down from New Jersey, and the plan is to have this thing right after the graduation ceremony. Now, as a father, you'd think I'd be right there alongside my wife, planning the details, just as excited as she was, right?

I nod my head at him while he looks at me for confirmation, and then he continues on. "Well, I'm not excited, he says. "For months I'd been acting scared to death, thinking about how I'm supposed to pay for this kid's schooling and everything. I got so wrapped up in the thought of finances, that I started scheduling myself doubles, trying to collect whatever I could to sock away. So, the day of the ceremony and the big party afterward? I missed all of it.

"You didn't! I say, completely enraptured by the story. Buck grins at me, almost shame-faced, and nods his head.

"I hadn't told my wife, either. She just assumed I'd taken off. When I was getting ready to head out the door, she stopped me and asked me where I thought I was going, and I told her *somebody's gotta pay for all this shit,* and left. I don't know what I was thinking, firing off at the mouth like that, especially toward this woman that had put up with my sorry ass for half my life. She kept her game face on throughout the ceremony and party, but once all the family members left, she absolutely unloaded on me. It was a fight."

"Damn, Buck! How'd you end up getting through all that?"

"Patience," he responds. "At first, anyway. I gave her space, let her say everything she needed to say. Right or wrong, my ass wrote a check, and she cashed it. I made myself miserable for about a month or so, trying to do right by her, but when I felt like it was taking too long for her to thaw out, I went ahead and put the gas pedal down."

"What'd you do?" I ask him, and he smiles as he recalls the events.

"I walked into the bedroom one night, went into her closet, grabbed a dress I thought she looked good in, and threw it on the bed. I said *Put that on, because we're going out. You've been so busy remembering why you're pissed at me that pretty soon you're gonna forget why you married me, and I'm not having any of that.* She tried to tell me no, but when she saw me putting the three piece suit that I hadn't worn in almost a decade, her curiosity got the better of her. She put on the dress, and I took her to the dance club we'd gone to when we were newlyweds. The place had changed a bit, but I slipped the DJ a twenty dollar bill and had him play our favorite song from when we first started dating. I took her out on the dance floor, and by the end of the song, we were back on the road, and the driving was *smooth,* if you catch my drift."

"Wow, Buck, who knew you had moves like that?" I say, stunned by the end of the story. He just shrugs his shoulders, though, and tells it to me plainly.

"It's not about having moves, Jimi. All I needed to do was

remind my wife why she fell in love with me in the first place. Every man ought to get the opportunity to do that, and if their wife or their girlfriend won't give them that opportunity, then they just need to *make* that opportunity, you know what I mean? I don't think too highly of Harris Crockett, and his wife can probably do better, but there must've been a reason they got married in the first place, right? Hopefully Harris figures that out quick, and tries to remind his wife of what that reason was. If she's good enough to him to call his workplace just to try and track him down, then I don't know how much better *he* can do. If he's not careful, he's liable to mess up one of the only good things he's got going on in life.

***

When my shift ends, I get my phone and shoot Stefania a text.

"You home?

"Yes. Why?

"Coming over today. Have something to give you.

She sends me a response that's just three question marks, but rather than keep it going, I leave it at that and go back to my apartment to get myself cleaned up. I shower, shave, and fix my hair so that I look as presentable as I can be. When I go to my closet, I get the nicest pair of pants I have with the fewest wrinkles, shake them out, and put them on. I grab a black belt, black shoes, and the only white button up shirt I own. Then, just as I'm about to shut the closet door, I see Arturo's grey tie hanging on a hook in the back. I take it and examine the blood stain that's now brown, aged, and looks set in.

"I can fix this, I mutter to myself, and I grab my phone, look up directions on how to get dried blood out of clothes, and then take the tie into the bathroom where I keep a bottle of hydrogen peroxide. Twenty minutes later, I'm dressed, standing in front of the bathroom mirror, and tying the tie that's now much cleaner than it was, save for a wet spot that's still lingering near the bottom.

From there, I throw on the only sports coat I own, inherited from Pop-Pop Mercier's closet from when I was big enough to fit into it. It's light brown and doesn't exactly match the outfit, but it's enough to help make the statement. There's a point I want to get across to Stefania, and there are several things I need to do to get it done. The suit is just the first part of it.

Once the jacket's buttoned, I leave the apartment, get in my car, and drive over to the bank. On the way, I call my mother, ready to share with her my big plan. The phone rings several times, but she never picks up. Instead, her voicemail comes on.

"Sorry you missed me. Leave a message."

Once I hear the beep that follows, I leave her a voicemail that goes differently than I planned. Instead of a recording of what my plans were, I leave her a message that's a little more direct, and meaningful. "Hey, Mom, it's Jimi. I know you're probably out somewhere, living your life or whatever. You don't have to call me back. Just wanted to tell you I love you. You're a better mother than I've given you credit for."

Happy with those words, I hang up and slide the phone into my back pocket. When I get to the bank, it's nearly empty, probably because it's still early in the day and not even ten o'clock yet. It takes no time to get help, and a middle-aged woman greets me with a smile from behind a glass partition and asks me what she can do for me today.

"I recently opened up a college savings account with you guys," I tell her, and I slip her the bank card from my wallet with all of the account information on it. She examines it, punches in some numbers, and then hands the card back to me through the partition.

"Yes, I see," she says. "And what would you like to do with that?"

"How do I go about adding someone to that account?" I ask her, and she reaches down into a little filing cabinet next to her desk, rifles through a few folders, and then pulls out a piece of paper and hands it through the partition.

"You just need to fill out this form, which basically gives the person permission to access the account, allowing them to put money in and take money out, though honestly you don't want to take any money out since it's designed to be a savings account.

"Right, I tell her. "The plan is to wait at least another eighteen years before anything gets taken out.

"Very good, sir, she says with a smile. "You just have the person fill out that paper with you, have it notarized, and then bring it back to me, and you should be all set.

I examine the paper, with all the legal words and the places to number, initial, and sign, feeling just how *adult* it is to have this kind of document in my hands, then fold it in three and tuck it inside my jacket pocket. "Thank you very much, ma'am, I tell the woman. "You've been very helpful today.

The last stop I make before I drive over to Stefania's place is the supermarket where I last bought her flowers. Knowing full well what I'm going to do, I walk briskly over to the floral area, grab the nicest looking bouquet of red roses, and walk over to the check-out aisle. Sure enough, the same guy the checked me out last time is working this aisle, and lays the same line on me as last time.

"For me? he says, "You shouldn't have.

"So what do red roses mean? I ask him, and he looks at me blankly for a second, like he doesn't remember having sold me the dozen yellow more than a month ago.

"That's simple, he responds, adopting a very serious tone that's in contrast to the bouncing quality he had when he laid down the *for me* shtick. "Red roses are for love, man; the passionate, longing kind.

"Good to know, I tell him, and the smile returns to his face.

"Did you get the right kind then? he asks.

"I'm hoping so, I say, and leave the supermarket with the flower stems wrapped up in a grocery bag to keep them from drying out.

It's just shy of eleven when I pull up to Stefania's apartment.

Her brother isn't there, and I am thankful for that. If he thought me asking his sister to listen to a Santana song was corny, who knows what he'd say about what I'm going to do next.

I get out of the car, inspect my clothes one more time, pat out any new wrinkles I see in my pants, and then approach the apartment door with flowers in hand. I give three loud knocks, step back, and take a deep breath, waiting for the door to open. A few seconds pass, I feel a spike in my nerves, and then I hear the sound of a chain lock sliding back, and the pop of a bolt being released.

Stefania opens the door, sees me, and then almost closes it immediately. Her hair looks like a wild mess; she's wearing sweatpants and a shirt that's about two sizes too big for her, and her face is as natural as the day she was born, without a trace of makeup to cover a single blemish.

"*¿La plena?* she says, exasperated, "Why are you dressed like that?

"I wanted to look nice for you, I tell her, and she rolls her eyes.

"What are you doing here, Jimi? she asks me. "I'm clearly not ready for company, and besides that, I don't know if I want to see you yet or not.

"I know that, I say, "But I wanted to give you something anyway.

"Roses? she says. "Really?

"Really, I answer, and I hand them to her. She begrudgingly accepts them at first, but then holds them up to her nose, smells them, and a small smile breaks over her face.

"I also got you something else, I tell her, and a look of panic spreads across her face as he watches me reach inside my jacket pocket.

"Oh, Jimi, no, she says, "Please don't do this.

When I remove the paper, her expression shifts from worry to confusion.

"You weren't expecting a ring, were you? I ask.

"You had me going there for a second, she says, and her look of curiosity deepens when she accepts the paper and reads over it. "What is this supposed to be? she asks.

"It's just a paper that says you get access to the account I opened up, I explain.

"Account for what? she responds, and when I tell her about opening up a college savings account for our child with the extra money I'm making, her face breaks a little, and she turns her back on me for a second to collect herself.

"What are you *doing* here, Jimi? she repeats, but now her voice sounds like she wrestling with something bigger, and so I open up and tell it to her.

"When I would go out and meet up with girls at bars and stuff, I explain, "I would do this thing where I'd ask them an open-ended question to make it seem like I was curious about their life and stuff, and that I was sensitive or whatever. Really, I was only asking them because I knew they'd ask me the same question after they'd answered it, and I usually had a response ready to go that was supposed to make me look good, or something like that.

Her look clouds over for a second, and a hint of anger exists in her voice when she asks, "Why are you telling me this.

"I'm telling you this, because I want to be honest with you, I say. "About being a bad guy before, but also about doing this thing where I've already planned out what I've wanted to say. I know what I want, but I don't want to have to play games with you or try to maneuver you into a conversation to say what I want to say. I want to treat you better than that and just tell you what I want.

"So what do you want? she asks me, and I tell it to her in the plainest terms possible.

"I want to remind you of why you fell in love with me, I answer. "I figure I've got four or five months left before the baby comes, and that's four or five months to show you that I really do care about you, the baby, and even your brother. I'm not asking you to marry me or anything; just let me build on what you liked about me when we first met. That's what I want.

"And how are you gonna build on it? she asks scornfully. "Are you going to try wine and dine me, or win me over with flowers, she says, brandishing the bouquet. Then she adds, "Are you going to buy me *breakfast*? It's a pointed question, but the effect is lost on me. I know what I want.

"Honestly, I answer, "I just want to do your dishes.

"What? she asks, and a hint of confusion has crept back into her voice. It's probably not the response she was expecting, and she looks unsure of what's next, staring me down like she's trying to make a judgement.

"That's how we started, isn't it? I explain. "Just the two of us cleaning up a mess? Kids are messy, Stef. You're gonna get tired. I just want to show you that I can still do your dishes. I could even fold your laundry, if you'll let me.

"Yeah? she asks me, and it looks as if something's ready to break inside of her.

"Yes, I tell her. "Please.

She pauses for a second, looks thoughtfully at me, and when she speaks again, her words sound confident, and final. "Okay.

She turns around, walks inside, and leaves the door open. Without hesitation, I step forward and follow her into her apartment, and I make sure to close the door behind me.

Acknowledgements

A great thanks is owed to the many people who spent some time with the book and gave me help along the way, and I'd like to recognize a few of them now:

Nick Johnson – for keeping me honest.

Danielle Rice – for enthusiastically reading the first draft.

Daniel Schwartz – for the due diligence that made a second draft possible.

Chasi and Cameron – for keeping my heart full and allowing me a happy place to write.

I thank you all.

About Christopher L. Malone

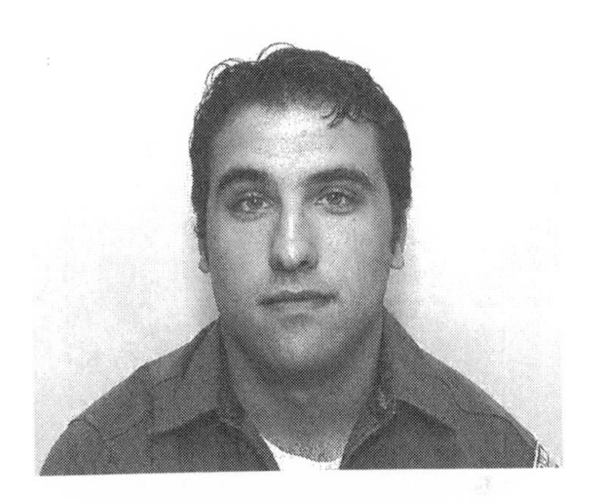

Christopher L. Malone is a Maryland writer who greatly enjoys spending time with his wife and son when he isn't too busy with school work or playing music.

In addition to teaching English, he's written several short stories that have been featured in online and print literary magazines, including The Dark City Crime and Mystery Magazine and The Literary Hatchet.

This is his first novel, and he's currently working on the next story.

Feel free to follow @CLMalone84 on Twitter for updates on his progress!

Available worldwide from

Amazon

79547654R00109

Made in the USA
Columbia, SC
25 October 2017